Hogan swallowed hard and released his rifle. "Who the hell are you?" he demanded.

"Name's Edge."

"Who killed my buddy?" Hogan demanded, waving one of his raised hands to indicate the corpse on the ground.

"I owed him for killing my horse, feller. What do you want?"

"Shuddup!" Hogan snapped, not taking his eyes off of Edge's face. "You oughta know I'm a duly deputized lawman of the town of Democracy, so best you put up that rifle and explain yourself."

Edge tilted his Winchester slightly and squeezed the trigger. Hogan froze and seemed surprised that he felt no pain. There were two holes in the crown of his hat—front and rear. Even though the light of day was fading fast, Hogan saw the bright glitter of cold anger in the half-breed's slitted eyes, as the lever of his Winchester was pumped.

"Already explained myself, deputy," Edge said evenly. "I'm a man without a horse on account of your buddy shot him—and I aim to get justice."

Edge leveled his rifle and took careful aim . . .

WARNING

This story is not for
the faint-hearted reader.

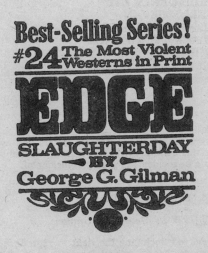

Best-Selling Series!

#24 The Most Violent Westerns in Print

EDGE

SLAUGHTERDAY
BY
George G. Gilman

PINNACLE BOOKS   LOS ANGELES

EDGE #24: SLAUGHTERDAY

Copyright © 1977 by George G. Gilman

All rights reserved, including the right to reproduce this book or portions thereof in any form.

A Pinnacle Books edition, published by special arrangement with New English Library, Limited, London
First published in Great Britain by New English Library Limited 1977

ISBN: 0-523-40-136-1

First printing, October 1977

Cover illustration by Bruce Minney

Printed in the United States of America

PINNACLE BOOKS, INC.
One Century Plaza
2029 Century Park East
Los Angeles, California 90067

Slaughterday

Chapter One

THE man cracked his eyes to the narrowest of slits against the driving rain and peered ahead. The black gelding beneath him continued to splash wearily through the hoof-deep mud of the trail. The wind veered away from the west and the rain fell with greater force, totally cutting off rider and mount from their surroundings. But the man was not given to seeing things which did not exist and he was certain he had seen a building crouched at the side of the trail: glimpsed it when, for no more than a second, the rain had slackened. The horse was newly purchased and not yet sufficiently familiar with the moods of his owner to sense the subtle change which had come over the man.

Horse and rider had covered another hundred and fifty feet of muddy trail when their rain-lashed private world was penetrated. The bullet made a hissing sound through the storm, punctuated by the crack of the rifle which had exploded it towards the man.

"Get outta here, Stanton man!"

"Dan, you don't know!"

The order had been snarled by a man. He had been cautioned by a woman, her voice shrill with fear.

"Name's Edge, feller!" the rider called—loud to be heard above the rainstorm but evenly pitched. "I'm my own man."

1

The gelding was army trained, so the rifle shot had not spooked him. He responded instantly to the tug on the reins, coming to an abrupt halt. Edge was self-taught and had been poised to meet trouble from the moment he had glimpsed the building through the curtain of slanting rain.

"Dan, it's a public road!"

There was no overt reason why a lone rider on a muddy Nebraska trail traveling through a cold and rain-soaked afternoon should have regarded the building with suspicion. Unless the rider happened to be the man called Edge, who had learned that survival depended upon expecting the threat of danger to become a reality at any moment from any quarter.

"Damnit, Laura. We ain't in no position to take chances!"

Edge had been holding the reins in just one hand since he saw the building. His right had been resting on his thigh, close to where the stock of a Winchester rifle jutted from the boot forward of his knee. The impassive set of his face had not altered and his posture in the saddle continued to be relaxed under the assault of the teeming rain.

What the horse had failed to sense was that, beneath the nonchalant exterior, the mind and muscles of the man had tensed for action and reaction.

The narrowing of the eyes gave no clue to this—had anyone been close enough to see. For, during the long ride from Fort Sully in the mid-Dakotas, Edge had been watchful every foot of the way. As he continued to be watchful now, moving only his eyes across his restricted field of vision while he listened to the man and the woman argue about how they should further respond to his unexpected appearance on the trail.

"But he's probably just an innocent traveler!" Laura pleaded.

Their voices remained loud, his still a snarl and the woman's losing some of its earlier shrillness. Edge's words were as evenly pitched as before, after he had turned to the side and spat in the same direction as the wind.

"Don't claim anything for me I'm not, ma'am!"

He doubted if they could see him. Once, they had. Maybe even more than once. When he had glimpsed the building? Or when another brief veering of the wind had revealed him to them while he had continued to be blinded to everything except the teeming rain? Perhaps in that instant Dan had got off the rifle shot. Edge chose to believe this and, in so doing, had to accept the man had purposely missed, aiming two feet above and to the left of his hat.

"Your name don't mean nothin' to us, stranger!" Dan snarled as Edge heeled the gelding forward again, at the same sluggish pace as before. "But you sure look like the type Stanton's been hirin'!"

"That's ridiculous, Dan," Laura challenged, her tone almost a snarl now. "You can't shoot a man because of what he looks like!"

Edge looked precisely what he was. Six feet three inches tall, he weighed close to two hundred pounds. He carried little excess fat and his flesh was evenly distributed to give him a lean, hard frame. The couple in the building would have received only a fleeting impression of his build, their view impaired by the weather and the knee-length coat which he wore. It was unlikely that they saw any detail of his face in such conditions over such a distance. If they had, perhaps Dan would have aimed the rifle shot to kill. For he was afraid, and the face of the man called Edge would not have served to ease his mind.

It was a face that drew features from a double heritage, passed on by a Mexican father and a Scandinavian mother. A face as lean as his physical build, with high cheekbones and a firm jawline. The eyes, which were deep-set under jutting brows, were of the lightest and clearest blue: never wide beneath their hooded lids and never looking warmer than winter ice, even in repose. The nose had a hawkish quality. The mouth was long, the lips narrow—suggesting, to those who cared to take note, the latent cruelty that had been instilled in the half-breed.

The skin—stretched taut over the bone structure—was dark brown, due in part to the Mexican blood coursing his veins. But a life spent almost entirely in the outdoors, exposed to every extreme of weather, had deepened the coloration even more. The network of lines which cut deep into the skin also had two sources. One was the passage of the more than thirty-five years which stretched out behind him. The second was the harshness of his existence during so many of those years.

Framing his face as he rode closer to the man with the rifle was the upturned collar of his coat and the pulled-down brim of his hat. Inside these was the jet black, shoulder-length hair, coarse textured and sheened: as much a physical characteristic inherited from his Mexican father as his ice blue eyes had so obviously been drawn from his northern European mother.

Heritage, the passing years, and countless experiences with evil had fashioned the face, the component features contributing to a whole that was sometimes regarded as handsome, sometimes ugly. The impression depended upon the preferences of the man or woman who drew it. In their present mood, Dan and Laura would surely see only the surface menace—heightened by a two-day growth of bristles—and might react instinctively.

So Edge moved his right hand from his thigh to the frame of the Winchester, not wanting to kill or maim but preparing himself to do so if events proved such an

4

action to be necessary for his survival. And, by the same token, he was just as capable of drawing back from the brink of violence if the actions of others allowed.

It had been that way since Dan shouted the threat . . . since Edge first saw the building through the rain . . . since even before he had come to be called Edge. For, although behind the viciousness that showed in his face and demeanor there was most definitely a killer, it was one who killed only from necessity, not by instinct.

"He's comin' closer, Laura!" the man in the building yelled, his voice rising to a shriek.

The wind continued to slant the rain forcefully out of the invisible sky. But the building acted as a weather break and the half-breed could see it now, its outline blurred by the rain which curled around its corners and over its roof. As Dan shouted, Edge reined in the gelding and eased his right boot out of the stirrup. His free hand gripped the saddlehorn and released the reins.

The place was a stage line way station, single story and L-shaped. Out back of the section facing the trail was a corral, the two sides not built on blocked off by fencing. The fence was broken down in several places. The building was in a bad state of repair.

Before the rainstorm the decrepit condition of the place would not have been so apparent. But now, many of the garishly printed posters which had been tacked up to cover almost every square inch of wall had been made sodden by water and then torn by the wind. They flapped under new assaults, and sometimes were ripped free and flung down to become pulp in the mud. The timbers that were revealed were cracked, warped, and rotted. There was not a pane of glass left in any window. The stoop had long ago collapsed to rubble. Out back, the stable doors facing on to the corral either lay

5

in the mud or swung and creaked on hinges, ready to be wrenched from the frames at any moment.

Edge saw the figures at a window at one end of the way station and tensed himself to the peak of readiness.

"The warning shot I won't hold against you, feller!" he called, concentrating on the window, watching for the slightest movement that might signal the need to make his move. "But I figure you've got a rifle aimed right at me now."

"You can bet your damn life on it, stranger!" Dan roared.

Edge nodded and his head was all that moved. "Best you know the score before you match me."

"Listen to the man, Dan!" Laura pleaded urgently.

Her voice sounded against the metallic scrapings of a repeater rifle being pumped, muted by the hissing rain.

The half-breed went on as if there had been no interruption. "Don't like having a gun aimed at me, feller. If there's the time, I always give folks that one warning. Coming in out of the wet now. If you want to point that rifle at me, you'd better want to squeeze the trigger."

"I can plug him, Laura!" Dan shouted, supremely confident. "I got a clear shot."

"Please!" the woman gasped.

"My life against yours," Edge said, and touched his heels to the flanks of the gelding.

The slow plod through the sucking mud began again, but this time the horse was unsettled: perhaps made nervous by the voices calling through the rain, or the fact that his rider was using only one stirrup and not holding the reins.

"You're not a Stanton man, are you?" Laura de-

6

manded. "We don't want any trouble with somebody who means us no harm!"

"Mean to kill the feller with you, ma'am," Edge replied. "If he's still pointing the rifle at me."

He had reached the most dangerous point of his approach now. The enveloping curtain of rain was too far behind him. The solid cover of the way station was more than a rifle shot in front of him. He was afraid, but the emotion was controlled: to an extent where he could harness it and use it to power extra speed of reflex action.

From their voices, it was obvious that the man and woman in the way station were hampered by a different brand of fear. They were as scared of the results of their own actions as of the tall, calm half-breed moving slowly towards them.

"No!" the woman shrieked.

There was a flurry of movement at the window and Dan roared an obscenity.

Edge lunged sideways out of the saddle, pushing with his left foot and left hand and wrenching the Winchester from the boot.

Dan's rifle exploded a second shot while the half-breed was in midair and pumping the Winchester action. He glimpsed the muzzle flash and knew he would not hear the hiss of the bullet through the rain. For the spurt of flame revealed the gun was angled up towards the drenching sky.

Dan cursed again and Laura screamed.

Edge hit the soft ground, the impact sending up a spray of mud in every direction. The gelding was not perturbed by the further discomfort of wetness against his coat.

"It's all right!" Laura roared. "It's all right, mister! I've got the gun!"

Edge had rolled, covering himself from hat to boots in

clinging mud. He rose to his knees and one hand, holding the rifle high, then unfolded fast to his full height. As the woman ended her panicked assurance, the half-breed exploded a shot. The bullet hit the timber above the window and penetrated its rottenness. Laura screamed as she was showered with sodden splinters.

Edge, the mud being washed from his face and clothing by the teeming rain, pumped the action of the Winchester and sent a second shot toward the building. This time to the left of the window.

"He's murderin' us!" Dan yelled.

Edge levered a third shell into the breech and exploded it through the timber to the right of the window.

"I've got the gun!" Laura shrieked again.

"Give it to me!"

"No!"

The door beside the collapsed stoop was wrenched open and the woman raced out into the rain. The rifle was held high above her head, clasped in two hands.

"Look!" she yelled.

"Laura, come back! He'll..."

Dan had started out of the way station, but advanced only two paces before he pulled up short. The woman was already stock still, ten yards away. He looked from Edge to Laura and back again. Then, showing the depth of his conviction that he expected the half-breed to kill them, his mouth dropped open to gape wide in amazement. For Edge had sidestepped to his horse, leaned across the saddle, and booted the Winchester.

"Just this thing I have about guns being aimed at me," the half-breed supplied as he picked up the reins and led the gelding forward.

"But you could've killed us!" Dan snarled, stoking a new fury. "Blastin' at us the way you did!"

"Leave it, Dan," Laura said wearily, dropping her

8

arms and allowing the rifle to fall into the mud. "He didn't kill us, so leave it."

"Right, ma'am," Edge augmented. "All I did was show I don't just shoot off my mouth."

Chapter Two

For a moment, it seemed that every muscle in the woman's body had been drained of strength by her relief. But she managed to stay on her feet until the man reached her. Then she leaned gratefully against him. Dan swallowed hard as Edge drew near. He hugged the woman protectively. "Ain't much I can say, Mr. Edge." He spoke the name tentatively, as if unsure he recalled it correctly. "Except that decent folks learn not to trust nobody around Democracy."

Edge sighed wearily. "When a man's not got much to say, best he keeps quiet after he's said it."

The man accepted the advice with a shrug of his shoulders. The woman, her shock diminished, became abruptly sullen and looked ready to snarl a retort.

"Let's get inside out of the rain," Dan urged, and turned to shepherd her back toward the doorway of the building.

"Worth saying and doing," Edge allowed, but did not follow them. Instead, he led the gelding around the side of the way station, through a break in the corral fence, and across to the stable block.

It was just a shell, malodorous with the stinks of decay. All the one-time fittings had been taken away, and rain poured in through several holes in the roof. But the walls kept out the full force of the wind and he was able to tether the horse in a corner that was relatively dry. He didn't unsaddle the animal and carried just a waxpaper-wrapped package of food and his Winchester across the corral.

Up close to the way station and no longer suspicious of what it contained, he glanced disinterestedly at those posters which were still readable. The name DEMOCRACY was prominent on each of them and all were designed to attract votes for various candidates in a forthcoming election. SNYDER for Mayor. BAILEY, MEEK, GRANT, McQUIGG and SWAN for town councillors. All the men were claiming to seek office on the liberal ticket. No opposition parties were represented on any of the posters.

Edge entered the way station through the rear door.

"If you won't listen to an explanation, at least accept an apology from my husband, Mr. Edge," the woman snapped at him. "And share a meal with us?"

They were sitting on piles of dislodged timber in front of a potbellied stove. The woman was fumbling through the contents of a carpetbag while her husband attempted to light a fire in the stove. Away from the driving rain, there was still enough light left in the late afternoon for Edge to see clearly the couple and his surroundings. The daylight came in through the window on the leeward side of the building. All the other windows were boarded up.

"Our name's Warren, Edge," the man mumbled, glancing up only briefly from his chore. "Laura and Dan. Sorry I acted so nervous awhile back."

"If it was an act, it was a fine performance, feller," the half-breed answered wryly. "But I don't want any other part of your play."

Warren snapped up his head to glare at Edge now. "We ain't about to ask any favors, mister! If you want ..."

11

His wife put a restraining hand on his arm. "Leave it, Dan. You've apologized and I've offered to make amends the best we can. Enough has been said."

The man was about forty. Once well built he was now running to fat. He had short-cropped blond hair above a fleshy face that was very pale. His wife was at least five years his junior. She was a fine-looking redhead with a slender but generously curved body. They matched heights at around five feet six inches. And there were other similarities they shared: a recent veneer of hardness overlaying a long experience of easy living, expensively tailored clothes well past the time when they should have been replaced, a clumsiness in the way they went about their menial chores—all of it adding up to a general impression of a once rich couple reduced to hard times.

Edge found a piece of unrotted timber and placed it on the damp dirt floor in a corner, twenty feet from the stove. He sat down on the plank, leaned his rifle against the wall, and unwrapped the package on his lap. There was just jerked beef and sourdough bread, but plenty of it. He ate sparingly though—as he always did when he could not be sure where the next meal was coming from.

Like the stables, the way station was little more than a shell. But enough of the debris of decay remained to show how the place had once been. The rear had been given over to living quarters for the man who ran the place. The front section had been a combination office and waiting room where passengers could purchase tickets and kill time until stage departure. It had been a long time since a stage called at the station.

The half-breed's sodden, mud-stained clothes began to dry on him and the coldness of the Nebraska day became more apparent. Until Dan Warren succeeded in building a fire in the stove and its warmth went a long way to make the weather an unpleasant memory. Then

12

the damp clothing of all three occupants of the derelict way station started to steam.

The Warrens ate a meal of bacon and beans. And there were just the sounds of the rainstorm until the couple poured themselves seconds of coffee.

"Will you not even accept this?" the woman asked, getting to her feet and extending her steaming tin cup toward the half-breed. "A simple favor between passing strangers? With no need to feel beholden."

Edge had finished eating and had rewrapped what was left of his food before the Warrens began their meal. Then he had rested the back of his head against the wall and closed his eyes. He had not slept.

At first, his thoughts had been concerned with the beginnings of his strong feeling about guns being aimed at him. Nobody enjoyed the experience, of course. But few made such an issue of it as the man called Edge.

It had begun long ago, on an Iowa farmstead when he was very young. His bother Jamie was several years younger. They had been playing with their father's old Starr rifle and fate had decreed the older brother should be holding the gun when it discharged its single shot.

Jamie had not died. But he had been severely crippled for the remainder of what fate also decreed should be a tragically short life. His right leg shattered to the extent that he had to swing it forward with both hands in order to walk. From the day of the accident, when the man called Edge was still named Josiah C. Hedges, he had started to learn how to handle guns.

At first, his father was the teacher. Then, after their parents died, the older brother passed on his knowledge to the younger and continued to learn himself.

But he was still a simple Iowa farm boy. The War Between the States made him into a man. As a cavalry lieutenant and then captain for the Union, the skills

13

he had already mastered were honed and new ones were learned.

And, at the end of the war, as he rode away from Appomattox Court House he was much like the man now resting in the shelter of the abandoned stage line way station. But the future he envisaged as he rode out of the East and into the Midwest required none of the evil qualities he had developed on so many bloody battlefields. And he was willing—and still capable—to forget all the bad lessons he had learned.

Then he found the tortured and bullet-riddled corpse of his young brother—the flesh of Jamie providing a meal for buzzards beside the burning ruin of the Iowa farmstead.

In tracking down and taking his revenge against the murderers of Jamie, Josiah C. Hedges used every cruel and evil skill he commanded. In war, his uniform and a cause protected him from the consequences of such actions. In the uneasy peace, the law branded him a wanton killer. And he took the new name of Edge.

All that was long ago. Easy to recall because the memories of his family were always fresh in his mind. Since then, his life had been featured by one violent episode after another as he moved aimlessly across the always menacing landscape of half a continent. Sometimes he sought to determine an aim—and set out to achieve it with a resolute single-mindedness that brooked no interference from earthly forces.

But always he failed: when he attempted to return to what once had been his, when he married, when he tried to put down roots far from the land that was his birthright, and even when it seemed he was on the point of establishing the most tenuous of relationships with a fellow human being.

For the fate which had caused him to cripple his brother inevitably took another cruel twist. And the man

14

called Edge was forced to accept that he was not only a loner, but also a loser.

Each explosion of violence deepened the lines inscribed on his lean face and hardened his attitude toward his fellow man. Each improved his skills and the reflexes which set them in motion—the skills of a killer who unleashed his latent cruelty for the sole purpose of survival. Like a wild animal in an alien terrain.

For, when a man is destined to be denied the rights of a human being, he is faced with only two alternatives. To give up and to die or to fight for all that is left to him—life.

Edge had never once contemplated suicide.

As he rested in the warmth of the way station, he involuntarily revealed that he was not asleep by occasionally raising a hand to rasp the knuckles along the bristles on his jaw. And, during this period, he had sensed that he was under surreptitious scrutiny by the silent couple seated close to the stove. When he cracked open his eyes, Laura Warren approached him. Her gown under her long coat rustled as she walked. There was a faint, sad smile on her attractive face. Behind her, Dan Warren was grimacing.

The half-breed set his hat squarely on his head again and touched its brim. "Obliged, ma'am," he said, and took the mug.

Her smile expanded to one of mild satisfaction; then she swung around and returned to her seat before the stove.

"Dan and I feel the same way you do about such things, Mr. Edge," Laura said pensively. "Throughout our lives we have never asked anybody for anything. Thus, we have never felt in debt to others."

She pushed her splayed hands out towards the stove and stared in the same direction.

"Ain't him or us look like it got us anyplace good!"

15

her husband growled, peering sullenly at the driving rain through the glassless window.

"We'll get by," Laura Warren said with soft-voiced determination. Then she hardened her tone as she looked at him. "Provided we take things as they come and do not lose our heads."

Edge sipped the coffee. It warmed his belly and the aroma masked the dankness of his surroundings. It was the first since a dawn breakfast, for he had not made camp at midday, riding on through the storm in search of shelter.

He had headed into the Dakotas simply because he had seen a picture of Bismarck hanging on the wall of a hotel room in Omaha. Iowa had spread out from the opposite bank of the Missouri and he had thought of Jamie. He had married Beth in the Dakotas and he recalled the bitter memories of the manner of her dying. But he had moved north, aboard a riverboat, simply on the whim of seeing a picture.

He had not needed work, but fate ordained he should earn a thousand dollars on the trip north. Impassively, he realised that every cent would be earned in a bloodbath of violence. And so it had been. In more ways than one, it had been like refighting the war. He never reached Bismarck and at Fort Sully he lost the urge to go there.

So he invested some of his newly earned money in a horse and supplies and started the ride back south. Drifting and waiting for trouble to strike.

"All right, Laura. All right. Edge ain't rubbin' my nose in it. You called it right and nobody got hurt. I don't need you to keep on ..."

"I'm sorry," his wife said quickly, and again calmed him by resting a hand on his arm.

A new silence settled. And only Edge was comfortable

16

with it, impassively drinking the coffee. A loner in a group, content to think his own thoughts.

"You headin' for Democracy, Edge?" Warren asked suddenly.

"Figure I hold the same views as Tom Jefferson did that first July Fourth," the half-breed answered wryly.

Warren was confused and his wife came to the rescue. "Mr. Edge is attempting to be humorous, Dan," she explained wearily. Then, to the half-breed: "He means the town, as you well know."

Edge nodded and got smoothly to his feet. He moved to the stove and placed the empty mug on an unopened suitcase where the other dirty utensils had been put down. "He mentioned it before, ma'am. And I saw the posters."

The woman's nod was more emphatic. "There is going to be trouble in Democracy, Mr. Edge." She sighed. "But you're no stranger to that I would guess."

Edge retrieved the Winchester and his meager supplies.

"If you go to town, you'll hear me and Laura started the trouble," Warren said quickly, waving a hand at his wife as she was about to stop him. "Stanton and his crowd'll call us every dirty name they can lay tongue to. Want you to know none of it'll be true."

"Bear it in mind, feller," Edge promised as he started for the rear door.

"Listen to me, damnit!" Warren snarled, then moderated his tone when his wife shot an anxious look at him. "Laura could tell it better. She had a lot of fancy learnin'. Enough so she was smart enough to school-teach Indians one time. She don't care much what people think, though. Learned all I know from my Pa. And one of the things he taught me was to have respect in other folks' eyes. I care about things like that."

The half-breed had reached the door. Laura seemed

17

to be willing him to hurry and leave. But her husband was desperate to be heard. His anxious eyes raked the room. They hesitated for a moment on the mud-caked Winchester at his side. Then he shook his head and stared at the suitcase.

"Edge, there's seventy-five thousand dollars in there!"

He pointed a shaking finger at the case. His wife gasped. Edge halted at the door and glanced back, his eyes just short, glittering threads.

"Please!" the woman begged him.

"No sweat, ma'am. Found out a long time ago big money only buys trouble. And I get more than my fair share of that for free."

"It can buy . . ."

"Dan!" Laura shrieked, fury shining in her dark eyes.

"All right, all right!" Dan allowed. "But the money belongs to us, Edge. The spread Stanton and his crowd of crooked politicians took from us was worth twice that. In Democracy they'll tell you we stole the money. But we didn't take nothin' that wasn't ours."

Edge and the woman looked at him. Laura was still afraid of the consequences of his revelation. The half-breed remained impassive. Warren appeared to be boiling over with the need to amplify what he had said. But then he shrugged.

"Just wanted you not to get any wrong ideas about Laura and me, that's all," he concluded miserably.

"Leave it be, Dan," his wife advised with a sigh. "What's in the past is done. Water down the river. And Mr. Edge—"

The half-breed showed a cold smile. "Doesn't give a damn."

He had a hand on the doorknob when the rifle shot cracked. The report seemed to still the sounds of the storm for an instant.

"You in there!" a man bellowed. "Come on out the front with your hands high!"

The shot had been exploded out back and to the left, in the vicinity of the stable block. The order had been directed from the trail.

"Hogan!" Laura Warren rasped, gripped by terror.

"Get down!" her husband snapped.

Fear held her immobile. Warren spoke an obscenity and lunged forward, knocking her sideways off the pile of timber as he snatched up his Winchester.

"You hear me, you Warrens?" the same voice bellowed from out front of the way station. "Do it, or we come in shootin'."

"Crooked deputy!" Dan Warren growled towards Edge.

"It isn't his fight," Laura said, staying down on the dirt floor.

Edge had swung around to flatten himself against the wall. His hand was still curled around the doorknob.

"Hogan!" Another man, calling from the rear of the way station.

"Ed Robarts!" Warren hissed through clenched teeth as he went in a crouched run to the unboarded window.

"Yeah, Ed?"

"They had a horse! They ain't got it no more!"

The half-breed's response to the news was a tightening of his lips and a narrowing of his eyes.

"God, I'm sorry," Laura rasped, and covered her face with her hands.

"Feller named Robarts is about to feel the same way," Edge muttered.

"Come when I yell!" Warren snapped, and dived headfirst through the glassless window.

"Hogan, the side!" a third man roared. He fired a shot. The bullet cracked through the window, hit the top of the stove, and ricocheted up into the ceiling.

19

"Bastard!" Robarts snarled.

Edge turned the doorknob, dropped the package of food, and wrenched open the door. He swung on to the threshold, pumping the action of the Winchester.

A man was halfway across the corral, his running figure blurred by the wind-driven rain. He was angling from the stable doorway towards the corner of the way station.

A shot cracked out and a man screamed.

The running man skidded to a halt and started to rake his rifle around to aim at Edge. "You're not Warren?" he croaked in amazement.

"Hear I ain't even along for the ride," Edge rasped, and squeezed the trigger of the Winchester. He aimed for the man's right kneecap.

Another shot exploded an instant before the half-breed absorbed the recoil of his rifle. Ed Robarts was hit twice. The bullet from Edge's rifle shattered the target it was intended for. The second shell smashed into the side of his head. The impact knocked him hard to the right. He was rigid with agony as the fall started. And limp with death when he thudded into the mud. Blood, fragments of pulpy tissue, and splinters of bone gushed out through the massive exit hole in his right temple. The pelting rain quickly diluted the coloring to merge it with the dark mud.

Warren came racing around the corner of the way station, a final wisp of smoke leaving the muzzle of his Winchester.

"Laura! Laura! Now!"

He didn't wait to see if his wife was responding to his call. Nor did he glance towards Edge. He altered the course of his mud-splashing run only slightly, to angle towards a rear corner of the corral where a trio of horses were tethered to a leaning fence post.

The half-breed powered into a run of his own, away

from the threshold of the way station toward the doorway of the stable.

"Hogan!" a pained voice shrieked from the side of the way station. "I've been hit!"

"Where's Robarts?" Hogan yelled, half angry and half fearful. "Robarts, you okay?"

Edge reached the stable and merely glanced with a brief grimace at the black gelding. The animal lay in an inert and untidy heap, a stain of slick redness beginning narrowly at the right eye and spreading to cover completely one side of the head.

Then he turned, levering a fresh shell into the breech of the Winchester, and surveyed the corral. The wind was veering and gusting all the time now, as afternoon retreated before the advance of evening. By turns, parts of the corral or the entire area and the rear of the way station were either revealed or hidden by the teeming rain. Sporadically, he saw Dan Warren untie two of the horses from the fence post and lead them hurriedly across the corral. And he also caught brief glimpses of Laura. She emerged tentatively from the rear door of the way station. Then broke into an awkward run, her progress impeded by the length of her skirt, the mud, and the heavy suitcase she dragged with her.

"Hogan, I think I'm hurt bad!"

"Robarts? Where the hell are you, Robarts? Answer me!"

The Warrens came together in the center of the corral. The man wrenched the suitcase from his wife's grasp, boosted her up on to one of the mounts, and then swung up into the saddle of the other. He slid the Winchester into the boot, then leaned far down to pick up the case.

Edge watched stoically. Since the three-man posse had announced its arrival, Warren had handled the emergency with cool skill—totally at odds with his response when Edge had first shown on the trail. But this time his wife had not interfered with his play.

As he hauled up the suitcase and hooked the handle over his saddlehorn, Warren continued to be in control of the situation. Laura glanced anxiously around. Her fear explanded to near terror again when she saw the tall, lean figure in the stable doorway. But then Edge touched the brim of his hat and she recognized him. She looked ready to offer yet another apology, but the wind veered once more and sheets of slanting rain drew a veil across the corral. The sound of the water pocking into the mud covered the beat of hooves. When the wind direction shifted, all that was left at the center of the corral was the slumped figure of the dead Robarts.

Then: "They're gettin' away, frig it!"

Hogan's roar was followed by three rapid rifle shots. And then the man's curse betrayed that each of the bullets had missed the retreating targets.

"Frig you!" the injured man at the side of the way station snarled. "I'm bleedin' harder than it's friggin' rainin'!"

Edge waited, Winchester held two-handed across his belly, hooded eyes training their gaze on the far corner of the way station.

After awhile, he heard voices. But the two men were no longer shouting and he could not discern what they were saying through the hiss of falling rain. But a scream of pain and an answering curse reached him clearly. A few moments later, the two rounded the corner. One was supporting the other, the injured man trying to avoid putting his left foot to the ground.

"Robarts, frig it!" Hogan rasped, and relinquished his support of the other man to run towards the corpse.

The man with the wounded leg dropped hard into the mud, venting a string of obscenities.

"Quit complainin', goddamnit!" Hogan snarled back at

him as he crouched beside the corpse and craned his head to look into the death mask of a face. "All you got is a scratch, Danvers! Ed got his brains blown out!"

"So least he ain't friggin' hurtin'!" Danvers countered through clenched teeth.

Edge swung his Winchester to cover Hogan and stepped out into the rain. For several paces the storm hid him from the men. When it eased, Hogan was erect again. His back was towards Edge as he trudged through the mud towards Danvers.

"Gene ain't gonna like this!" Hogan growled.

"Save that worry for later, feller," Edge said evenly. Hogan whirled. Danvers leaned to the side to see around him. "I don't like it. And I'm here and now."

Hogan's Winchester was held in just one hand. He made a move to bring up the other one, but the rifle trained on his chest froze him. If Danvers had brought a rifle to the way station, he had discarded it when he was wounded. Both men, like the dead Robarts, were engulfed in long oilskin coats that made their holstered revolvers inaccessible. All three wore deputy's badges pinned to their coats.

Hogan swallowed hard and released his rifle. It splashed into the mud. "Who the hell are you?" he demanded, raising his hands up level with his shoulders.

They were broad shoulders and he looked like he had a powerful physique beneath the coat. There was a hardness in his fifty-year-old face, most of it visible in his small, dark eyes. His top lip was decorated with a bushy grey moustache.

"Name's Edge."

"You're with the Warrens?" Danvers snarled. He was in his mid-twenties. Short and lean with a thin face that was perhaps so pale because of his pain.

"I'm with me."

"Who did that to Robarts?" Hogan demanded, waving

one of his raised hands slightly to indicate the corpse. Robarts had died shortly before he was thirty. He had been almost classically good looking before death contorted his well-sculptured features.

"Owed him for killing my horse, feller. Tried to give him a painful memory about it. Warren made it so he'll never remember anything."

"What d'you want, mister?" Danvers rasped.

"Shuddup!" Hogan snapped at him, not taking his hard eyes off Edge's water-run face. "You oughta know I'm a duly deputized lawman of the town of Democracy and county of Carroll, Nebraska, mister! Same way Luke Danvers is. And Ed Robarts was. So best you put up that rifle and explain yourself."

Edge tilted the Winchester slightly and squeezed the trigger. Hogan yelled and took a fast step backwards. Danvers, who had started to pull himself upright against the way station wall, cursed and dropped into the mud again. Hogan froze and seemed surprised that he felt no pain. There were two holes in the crown of his hat—front and rear. But the lanyard, pulled tight against the wind, had kept the hat in place.

Even though the light of the dying day was fading fast, Hogan saw the bright glitter of cold anger in the half-breed's slitted eyes as the lever action of the Winchester was pumped.

"Already explained myself, deputy," Edge said evenly. "I'm a man without a horse. On account of your buddy shot him."

Hogan swallowed hard again. "Ed must have thought it was the Warrens'. We was here on official law business. Your loss'll be made good if it's proved you weren't aidin' and abettin' the Warrens."

Edge pursed his lips, then parted them slightly to show the white line of his teeth.

"Best you do like you told me and shuddup, Arnie!"

Danvers warned. "This guy ain't impressed by our badges."

"But your good sense is getting to me," Edge muttered, and raked the rifle around to cover the injured man sitting against the base of the wall. "You want to make him see some?"

"How?"

"If he does like he's told, the sheriff will only be mad about losing one deputy."

Danvers sucked in a deep breath.

"You want the horse, take it!" Hogan growled.

"Intend to. Didn't lose my gear though. Like for it to be put on my new horse."

Hogan made a sound of angry disgust deep in his throat.

"Do it, Arnie!" Danvers implored, staring fearfully at the muzzle of the aimed Winchester.

Edge flicked his gaze from one man to the other and back again.

"And don't try nothin', Arnie!" Danvers urged. "He's got a gun under the coat, mister. Same as I got. You want us to ditch them?"

"Want my gear on my new horse," Edge reiterated. "Just that."

"Arnie?"

Hogan hesitated for a long moment, then started toward the stable. "All right, mister. You win for now. But Carroll's a big county and you're gonna have to ride long and hard before you're clear of Gene Stanton's jurisdiction."

"Goddamnit, Hogan!" Danvers growled. "It's me your half-assed threats are scarin'."

But the older man had already advanced to the stable doorway to do Edge's bidding. The wind gusted and he was hidden by the weather. Edge moved slightly, to put his back to the way station wall. While he kept the rifle

25

trained on Danvers, he constantly moved his slitted eyes, dividing his attention between the hostage and the rain-lashed corral.

"Arnie's right, mister," the wounded man blurted out after a long, grim silence. "You ain't bein' wise, messin' with lawmen in Carroll County. Especially after it looks like you helped the Warrens get away from us."

During respites in the teeming rain, Edge glimpsed Arnie Hogan as the deputy brought the saddle and bed-roll from the stable: then removed the gear from the tethered horse and replaced it with that taken off the dead gelding.

"Had coffee with them, was all," Edge replied as Hogan led the piebald gelding through the mud of the corral.

Danvers spat between his legs. "Fat chance anyone'll believe that!"

"Ain't important, anyways," Hogan growled, releasing the reins and moving to stand beside the injured man. "You admitted to puttin' a bullet into a deputy in the lawful execution of his duty, mister."

"Yeah!" Danvers exclaimed, the fear draining out of him as Edge swung up into his own saddle on a strange mount. "And now you're stealin' a horse. Both them are hangin' crimes in this part of the country."

"Stanton the man I see to straighten things out?" Edge asked, holding the Winchester one-handed, aimed between the two men.

"You're goin' to Democracy?" Danvers gasped.

Hogan showed a harsh grin. "Don't try and talk him outta it, Luke."

Edge urged the piebald forward, to the corner of the way station. He kept his eyes and the rifle directed at the two lawmen. Hogan's Winchester was far out of reach in the mud and neither of the deputies made a move to go for their covered handguns.

"Do us a favor, mister!" the older man called lightly. "Ask Gene Stanton not to hang you until me and Luke get back to town."

Danvers laughed, then scowled as the shaking of his body triggered a fresh wave of pain in his injured leg. It soured his mood. "Hell, Arnie," he snarled. "We're kiddin' ourselves. This guy ain't fool enough to turn himself in on a hangin' rap. He'll be free and clear of the county by the time we flag down the Laramie stage and reach Democracy!"

"Damn it, you're right!" Hogan retorted as Edge heeled his horse out of sight around the corner of the way station.

Hogan powered away from the wall, raced through the mud, and scooped up his Winchester.

Grimacing against the pain, Danvers forced himself erect against the wall and delved inside his coat to draw a Colt revolver.

The wind curled over the roof of the stable block and hurled lashing rain across the corral.

Danvers staggered along beside the wall, cursing his wounded leg at every step. Hogan whirled and raced forward, pumping the action of his muddy rifle.

The wind eased and the rain slackened.

Both lawmen came to a halt.

Edge had wheeled his horse and ridden him clear of the corner. His Winchester was out of the boot once more.

Its first report blasted a bullet into the center of Hogan's face. The deputy was flipped on to his back. Spurting blood from out of his bushy moustache rose as high as splashing mud.

It was Danvers who screamed, and got off a shot from his Colt. But the rifle in the half-breed's hands had raked to the left and exploded a second shot as soon as the lever action was completed. Danvers's bullet went

27

high and wide. He was flat against the wall then, and starting a slide down into the mud. A large stain blossomed larger on his chest.

"Why?" he croaked, his legs splaying through the mire of the corral as his rump settled.

"Figure you fellers were trying to kill me," Edge answered evenly, booting the Winchester.

"You could have got free and clear." Death was taking its initial grip on the face of Danvers.

"Intend to have my say in Democracy, feller. Just smoothing the way to being believed, is all."

Danvers's eyes stayed open. A final breath flooded blood over his dropped lower lip. His head fell forward to rest his chin on his chest. He stayed sitting against the wall.

Edge wheeled the piebald as he muttered: "And death's the great leveler."

Chapter Three

HALF a mile south of the derelict way station with its corpse-littered corral the trail forked. Blistering summers and harsh winters in the Nebraska high country had faded the lettering on the signboards nailed to a leafless elm. But it was just readable. The trail which curved off to the west led to Laramie, across the state line in Wyoming Territory. Due south lay Democracy.

There were several other elms standing tall and erect in the fork of the trails. Those sheltered from the full force of the storm continued to support posters bearing the same names as those back at the way station. All were printed in a familiar red.

Edge, his eyes cracked against the rain which by turns slanted in from the west and southwest, kept the piebald headed for Democracy. He was fully aware of the truth which Luke Danvers had repeated in the final seconds of life. He could have allowed the two deputies to live, ridden in any other direction, and been free and clear before a pursuit could be organized.

But that was not the half-breed's way. Despite the fact that he had killed countless men before Hogan and Danvers dropped into the mud in front of the blasting Winchester, he was wanted by the law for only one crime. As ex-Captain Josiah C. Hedges, he had killed a man named Elliot Thombs in the state of Kansas while he was tracking the murderers of Jamie.

The wanted flyers were still out on him for that and once, long ago, a lawman with good reason to hate Edge had almost made him pay for the ancient crime.

As always, the half-breed learned from experience. Trouble dogged him or lay in wait for him. For the most part, he could do nothing to avoid it—except where the law was concerned. Which was the reason he took the trail to Democracy.

With the coming of full night, the wind dropped and the rain eased off. The cloud-heavy sky remained hidden and visibility was extended only a few yards. But the lone rider deliberately heading for one brand of trouble to avoid a worse kind was able to see the trail more clearly now. By the same token, he knew that others would be able to spot him over a greater distance. So he moved his head constantly, peering in every direction. He saw trees and rocks and the fringes of waterlogged meadows. Here and there, election posters, still in place or in shreds on the ground.

A man with a more vivid imagination than Edge might have sensed menace in the rain-shrouded night. The red ink of the posters might have reminded him of the blood which had spurted from the bodies of the lawmen. And he might constantly have relived the first shot to hiss through the storm.

But the half-breed was too much of a realist. One of the skills he had learned at war was the ability to detect danger before it struck at him. Sometimes it was like a sixth sense, particularly when he was asleep. Mostly, though, it was manifested through a physical clue—as when he had first seen the way station.

For such a faculty to be of use, his mind had to be clear of conjured figments of imagination. So he heard the sounds of the rain and the progress of the gelding

30

for what they were. And his eyes identified the natural formations of the landscape without reading into them anything which did not exist.

The clang of the bell did not startle him. The piebald gelding pricked his ears and would have moved into a faster step had Edge given him free rein.

"Almost home, uh?" the half-breed muttered.

The bell sounded its same note six times before Edge reached the town marker. And six more times to signify the time of midnight, as he read the sign: DEMOCRACY WELCOMES YOU—Population 750—Elevation 2500 feet.

It was an early-to-bed town. The open trail became a broad street, flanked by frame buildings standing behind covered sidewalks. No lights showed anywhere until Edge had ridden between the buildings for about a hundred yards. At intervals, he passed over plank walkways, connecting one side of the street to the other, and under canvas signs urging the citizens to vote for Snyder, Bailey, Meek, Grant, McQuigg, and Swan.

At the center of town, a cross street formed an intersection and a row of six windows gleamed with lamplight. The buildings stretching away on the north-south street and those on the one which ran east to west were as dark as those Edge had already seen.

He angled the piebald across the intersection toward the entrance of the lighted building on the southwest corner. It was brick built and two stories high. The entrance was angled on the corner and a stylishly painted sign above the double closed doors proclaimed: PALACE HOTEL. The place had a frontage on two streets and all the lighted windows were on the first floor, facing the cross street.

Edge swung the horse lengthwise to the angled porch of the hotel so that he was able to dismount on to it, his booted feet finding solid timber instead of mud and the

31

roof giving him shelter from the rain. As he unsaddled the piebald, the only sounds in town were of rain hitting flat roofs and gushing over the eaves to splash down walls.

The animal was still anxious to be given his head and, when Edge slapped him lightly on the rump, he backed away, turned, and trotted into the rainy darkness of the main street's north section.

The half-breed unbuttoned his long coat before he pushed open one of the two doors and carried his gear into the Palace Hotel.

"Be lyin' if I said good evenin' to you, stranger."

The man who spoke the greeting was tall and thin and grey-haired. He sat on a hard-seated, straight-backed chair in the center of a large lobby. In front of him was an easel supporting a half-finished canvas in oils. The grey-haired man had a palette in one hand and a brush in the other. His subject was a young Negro in a lounging pose on a deeply upholstered sofa six feet in front of him.

"You want a room, mister?" the Negro asked with a broad grin of pleasure.

"You just hold still a while longer, Conrad," the artist snapped, adding another brush stroke to the canvas.

There was a rush mat inside the entrance. Edge dripped water on to it as he glanced around. The lobby had a polished wooden floor, paneled walls, and a high ceiling washed in white. Kerosene lamps burned on wall brackets. An ornately banistered stairway canted up one side. A carved desk ran along the rear. Open double doors across from the stairs gave on to a long saloon, brightly lit but empty. The place looked like the entrance to some big-city hotel.

"You gotta do somethin' before you do anythin' else in Democracy, stranger," the grey-haired man drawled, still concentrating on his painting.

32

He was a fine draftsman, the work he was engaged on being an exact copy of its subject. Several other oils in the same style were hung on the walls of the lobby—portraits, full-length figures, and landscapes. All of them were neat and tidy and totally lacking in life.

"I already rode from the town marker to here," Edge answered, starting towards the desk. The water dripping from his clothes and gear made a louder sound hitting the polished wood.

The grey-haired man was neat and tidy and lacking in any animation beyond that required to work on the painting. He was about sixty, an inch over six feet tall, and probably weighing no more than a hundred and twenty pounds. His hair was neatly trimmed and sheened by pomade. His hollow-cheeked, high-foreheaded face was clean shaven and talced. His green eyes looked dead and he hardly moved his thin lips when he spoke. He was dressed in a city suit, white shirt, bootlace tie, and polished shoes. He had not got wet reaching the lobby of the Palace Hotel.

"That's because it's late and you weren't expected, stranger. Otherwise, you'd have had your guns taken from you at the town limits."

"This gent's Gene Stanton, mister," the Negro supplied. "Sheriff of Democracy and the whole of Carroll County."

Edge had reached the desk. He loaded his gear on to its highly polished top and turned to lean his back against it.

Stanton interrupted his work for long enough to hold open his suit jacket and display the five-pointed tin star pinned to his matching vest.

The half-breed nodded. "Wouldn't have been you who took them, I guess?"

"This gent's got deputies workin' for him, mister," the Negro answered. He was about twenty with a handsome

33

face and solid, strong-looking build. He was dressed in sharply pressed pants, a vest, shirt, and necktie. All the clothes seemed to be too tight and too short for his five-foot-nine height and bulky frame.

"Ain't the normal rule, stranger," Stanton explained, back working again. "But it's election time. Feelin's are runnin' a little high. My view about keepin' the law, prevention's better than cure. You want to set your rifle and gunbelt down here on the floor by me, stranger? Then Conrad'll check you in the hotel. Done enough paintin' for one night, I reckon."

The Negro vented a low sigh of relief.

"Hold still!" Stanton snapped at him as the subject turned his head to look towards Edge.

Conrad resumed his pose fast, but not before he had time to see the glitter in the half-breed's eyes and recognize what it signified.

"Best everyone in Democracy does like this gent says, mister. He's got some real tough helpers."

The comment persuaded Stanton to look at Edge for a second time. Harder and longer than when he had glanced at him as the door closed. The green eyes did not lose their dead look. But his expression altered from vacant to menacing by a mere curling back of the thin lips over teeth too perfect to be natural. The lawman talked between the clenched teeth.

"You look tough, stranger. And I guess that's what you are, right enough. But you better listen to what Conrad Power tells you. Or get on your horse and ride out of Democracy."

The Negro decided he could move without arousing Stanton's chagrin now. He got up fast from the sofa and hurried across the lobby to get behind the desk. It was familiar territory to him and he looked at ease there.

"I ain't armed, stranger." The sheriff was not afraid. Merely stating a fact.

34

"Nor got any helpers close by, seems to me," Edge answered.

"Told you—prevention's better than cure." He slotted his brush into the palette, stood up, and placed the materials of his hobby on the chair. "Conrad here'll bear witness I tried it with you, stranger." He nodded to the Negro. "Check him in."

He had a gangling, easy walk for a man of his years. It carried him nonchalantly across the lobby and up the stairs. Halfway to the top, a woman stood aside for him to pass. He ignored her and she grimaced at his retreating back.

"You're lookin' for a room, feller, I got the best one in the house," the woman called cheerfully as she reached the foot of the stairs. "Course, it comes at a higher rent—on account of the extras a man gets in it."

She had jet black hair that flowed softly to her shoulders. It was the only soft thing about her. Her thirty-year-old face was basically pretty, but she lost the effect by using too much paint and powder in an attempt to add sensual allure to her features. She was short, and probably plump—but boning beneath the tight bodice of her high-necked, long-sleeved, flame-red gown forced her body into the too rigid lines of conical breasts and nipped waist. She walked with an accentuated sway of her hips and did a graceless pirouette before coming to a halt.

"Fay Reeves, mister," Power announced without enthusiasm. "Resident whore of the Palace Hotel."

"Figured she might be," Edge muttered. He touched the brim of his hat to the woman and stifled a yawn as he turned to the desk. "Any room but hers. Only extra I'll pay for is a bath."

The Negro was dividing his attention between Edge and the balcony at the top of the stairway. But his

35

hands were fumbling beneath the desk and he came up with the register and a key.

"Been a long, hard day, uh feller?" the whore asked. Then forced a girlish giggle. "I can top it with a long, hard night. If you know what I mean."

Power did some more fumbling under the desk and produced a pen and inkpot. He was concentrating entirely on the balcony now. When footfalls sounded up there, his hands shook. Edge had to take the key from him to see that it was labeled with the numeral seven. Then he turned the register, opened it, and filled out his name, adding the number of his room.

Fay Reeves had started the forced giggle again, but curtailed it. Edge dropped the room key in a shirt pocket, lifted his gear, and turned.

Sheriff Gene Stanton was descending the stairs. He had donned a black stetson, yellow oilskin coat, and knee-high overshoes. Again he ignored the suddenly nervous whore and the equally anxious Negro clerk. But, at the double doors, he looked over his shoulder to fix Edge with his dead-eye stare.

"Don't get too comfortable here at the Palace, stranger. Pretty soon you'll be roomin' as a guest of the county."

Then he stepped outside and closed the doors firmly behind him. His footfalls on the sidewalk were soon masked by the falling rain.

"You crossed up that bastard?" the whore exclaimed, eyeing Edge in a new light. Her blue, paint-encircled eyes showed an odd mixture of admiration and pity.

"Wouldn't give the gent his guns," Power supplied.

She shook her head. "Feller, did you just ask for trouble."

"Just held on to a couple of ways of handling it is all," the half-breed answered. "Room upstairs?"

Power glanced at the register. "Yes, mister. First door

on the right. Overlooks Main Street and Union Square. I'll fix you a tub and some hot water, mister. But, like the gent says, don't you get too comfortable in there. He ain't never said he'd do nothin' without he didn't do it."

"First time for everything," Edge replied.

"And a last," the whore countered. "Best a man dies in bed than in a bath—if you know what I mean."

She put her hands on her hips and swung sideways on from the waist, to present the profile of her stoutly supported upper body to the half-breed.

"And I guess they'll have to kill you to take you, uh mister?" Power asked. It was obvious from his expression that he regarded the outcome as inevitable.

"So I figure I just need the one fight on my hands," Edge told the whore as he stepped around her.

She looked confused. Then giggled. "I can be took real easy, feller. All you got to do is pay the price and I surrender."

Edge halted briefly and looked her up and down, his mouthline betraying the hint of a smile.

"Give you a real hot time, feller," she encouraged.

"Can see how I could work up a sweat, ma'am," he answered as he formed a fist and flicked his forefinger away from the thumb. The nail made a sharp sound against the boned undergarment beneath the bodice of her gown. "Looking for a chink in your armor."

Chapter Four

THE Palace Hotel was not all front. The stairway, the
balcony, and the hallways leading off it were all carpet-
ed. There was matting on the floor of room seven,
which was additionally furnished with a double bed,
two winged chairs, a bureau, and a clothes closet. Two
landscape pictures which had obviously been painted by
Democracy's sheriff hung on the walls.

The rain had stopped now and although the moon
was just a pale three-quarter orb behind thick cloud,
enough light filtered in through the net curtains hung at
the two windows of the room for Edge not to need the
lamp on the washed wall above the bed.

From the windows, he was able to look out over half
the town. It was as quiet as it had been when he rode
in, but now another building showed a light—halfway
along Main's north section, on the opposite side of the
street.

Edge dropped his saddle and bedroll in a corner of
the room, then added his topcoat and hat to the pile. He
moved one of the winged chairs against the wall opposite the door, sat down, and began to take shells from
his gunbelt and feed them through the loading gate of
the Winchester.

Before he had been in Omaha, where he saw the print
of Bismarck, he was in San Francisco. The hotel he

stayed in there was called the Palace. And a picture painted by a far superior artist to Stanton had been the motive for a great deal of killing.

Edge had done his share—as coldly as he had gunned down the two deputies back at the way station. But he was being paid to do a job then.

Today—yesterday and today, he was reminded as the town clock chimed the single note of a quarter after midnight—there was no money involved. Not for him, anyway. And, as Laura Warren had groaned at the start of the trouble at the way station, it was not his fight. Yet here he was, waiting in the gloom and cold of a strange hotel room, having made it his fight.

Knuckles rapped lightly on the door panel. He pumped the action of the rifle and glanced out through one of the windows. The panorama of that section of town was still deserted. The single light continued to shine.

"It's me," Fay Reeves called nervously. "I've got the tub."

"Guess you've been maid lots of times," Edge answered.

She opened the door wide and glowered at him through the dim light.

"I'm doin' a favor for Conrad, that's all."

She leaned behind her and dragged the tin tub across the threshold. Edge continued to sit in the chair, the Winchester resting across the two arms.

"You that whore with a heart of gold?"

She straightened and massaged the small of her back. "Feller, you made enemies enough crossin' words with that bastard Stanton. But you're lucky, too. I'm neutral. Conrad's gone to get you some help."

Edge did not reveal his surprise. "Just need some hot water to fill the tub."

She spat on the floor, then immediately regretted it

39

and spread the saliva with the toe of her shoe. "You're crazy, you know that? You don't know nothin' about this town. You want me to straighten you out—if there's time before you wind up dead?"

Edge glanced out of the window again, then did a double take. The north section of Main Street was no longer deserted. The light in the window continued to shine, but it was dimmer. Three men were moving away from it towards Union Square. The tall, oilskin-clad figure of Stanton was in the middle. He was flanked by men of lesser height but broader build. They were dressed Western style, coatless to show the holstered gunbelts slung around their hips.

"Want you to leave," the half-breed growled. "Company's coming and I've got my reputation to think of."

"For dyin' a fool?" she snapped.

"For not consorting with your kind. Beat it, whore."

She was not insulted. Merely dismayed. She opened her vividly painted mouth to say something, then turned and went out of the room, slamming the door behind her.

Edge glanced out of the window again and watched as the three men crossed Union Square and moved out of his field of vision in front of the hotel. He stood up then, and eased open the window. The room had never been warm but the outside air which streamed in was a great deal colder. He heard the footfalls of the men against the sidewalk, then the door opening. As soon as they were inside the lobby, he swung his legs over the sill to step on to the hotel porch roof. He closed the window, checked that a man had not been posted outside, and lowered himself to the sidewalk below.

When he reached the angled entrance of the hotel, a movement on the west section of the cross street caught his eye. Three people were crossing from one side to the other, ignoring the plank walkways and splashing through the ankle-deep mud in their haste.

Conrad Power's ebony face was sheened in the pale moonlight. He was leading the way and a man and a woman were struggling to keep up with him.

"Ain't exactly the Seventh Cavalry," the half-breed rasped softly, then opened one of the doors just wide enough to allow him to step through.

As far as he could tell, the approaching trio had not seen him. And Gene Stanton was not aware of him. For the door made no sound in opening and closing, and Edge's tread was silent on the rush matting inside the threshold.

The elderly sheriff had his back to the entrance and was studying his painting, head cocked to one side as he absently wiped his brush on a piece of rag.

"You in there!" a man snarled upstairs. "Edge! This is the law and you're under arrest!"

Edge stepped off the matting and on to the wooden floor. He purposely set his heel down hard.

Stanton snapped his head erect, then around. For a moment, his eyes did not look dead. He peered into the face of the half-breed and saw an index finger pressed to the lips. Then looked at the aimed Winchester, held in just one hand, an elbow supporting the stock to the hip. It took less than a second for the sheriff to appraise the situation and for that short time terror animated the green eyes. But he controlled it, before he swung his gaze up towards the balcony.

"Come out with your hands up, Edge! Or we come in shootin'!"

As the same deputy shouted the demand and threat, Edge spoke softly to Stanton, advancing on him.

"Death's like your view of the law, feller. Except there ain't no cure for it."

41

"You hear me, Edge?"

The half-breed motioned with the Winchester as Stanton looked back at him. The rifle was held two-handed now and the sheriff complied with its tacit order. Still holding the brush and the cleaning rag, he moved toward and through the open doorway into the saloon.

"Count of three, Edge!"

Inside the brightly lit saloon, the half-breed indicated Stanton should sit at a table with his back to the lobby.

"One!"

Edge sat down opposite the sheriff and rested the Winchester against his chair. Then he moved the chair slightly so that he had a clear view around Stanton into the hotel lobby. He draped his right hand over the jutting butt of his holstered Colt.

"Two!"

Two gunshots exploded the silence following the single word. A door crashed open and a window shattered.

"Seems a man can't trust the law in this town," Edge muttered.

More glass was smashed and footfalls pounded the floor of room seven. The deputy who had crashed through the door tripped on the bathtub and vented a curse as he went down.

"He ain't here!" This was yelled by the second deputy—the one who had followed his revolver shot in through the window. "Gene, watch out! He ain't in his room!"

"Nice when folks worry about you," Edge said.

"What's the idea?" Stanton croaked, raising a hand to wipe saliva off his lower lip.

"To stay alive, feller."

The deputies stormed out of the room as both entrance doors of the hotel were flung open and Power led his relief column into the lobby.

"Stanton!" the man with the Negro shouted breathlessly. "Stanton, if you've killed him there'll be hell to pay."

"How about if I get killed?" the lawman called flatly, not taking his dead eyes off Edge's face as the half-breed raised his left hand to tug at his earlobe. "What then, Lovejoy?"

The Negro pulled up short in the center of the lobby. Lovejoy and the woman slammed into him, one of them stumbling against the easel. It tipped and the still wet painting fell face forward on to the floor.

The two deputies came to an abrupt halt, halfway down the stairs. Their guns were still drawn but they did not bring them up to the aim as they leaned over the ornate banisters to stare through the doorway into the saloon. Every face expressed a mixture of anxiety and anger.

"Don't plan on killing anyone else," Edge announced, as the town clock chimed the half hour. "You want to tell your men to come on down, sheriff? But best they leave their guns on the stairs."

"You sure are one cool customer, mister," the Negro gasped.

"Cold's the word, feller," the half-breed corrected, continuing to tug at his ear. "As well as dirty, thirsty, and tired."

The two deputies were both in their early thirties. Scowls fitted well on their hard-looking faces. Lovejoy was a match for Stanton's age. But he was more than a head shorter and a great deal heavier. There was just a ring of sandy hair on the crown of his head. His skin was deeply wrinkled, the complexion ruddy. The woman was a homely forty-year-old, a brunette with a dumpy body. She had big brown eyes and an aggressive jawline. Both she and Lovejoy had obviously dressed hurriedly after Conrad Power roused them.

43

Edge moved his left hand slowly from his ear to the nape of his neck. For a moment, it was hidden under the thick fall of his long hair. When the hand reappeared, it was fisted around the wooden handle of a straight razor, with the point of the blade honed as sharp as the edge. The blade glinted briefly in the lamplight as the half-breed reached across the table.

"No!" Lovejoy shrieked.

The woman gasped.

Power's teeth gleamed white in a grin of pleasure.

The deputies swung their guns to the aim now.

Gene Stanton proved he was a brave man. He curled back his lips in a grimace, but did not attempt to move away from the razor as its point rested against his throat. The pulsing of the flesh became more rapid.

"Prevention's better than cure," Edge reminded.

"Gene?" the deputy with a squinting right eye called anxiously.

"Do like he says, Nugent. You, too, Forman. This man ain't no ordinary saddle-tramp."

Stanton watched Edge and the half-breed watched the two deputies. They straightened on the stairway, stooped to lay their guns on a tread, and came down. For a few moments, they were out of Edge's field of vision.

"You people come on in," the half-breed invited.

Conrad Power again took the lead and the three of them stood at one side of the entrance. The two deputies appeared in the lobby and at a nod from Edge took up a position on the other side. Then Edge grunted his satisfaction and leaned back in his chair, sliding the razor back into the leather pouch that was held at the nape of his neck by a beaded thong. Forman, the deputy with a pencil-thin black moustache, saw the move as an opening.

"Don't!" his partner, Nugent, growled.

Forman did a double take and saw the propped Winchester and the half-breed's right hand draped over the Colt butt.

"Right," Stanton confirmed, not taking his eyes off the face of Edge. "We've got nothin' to lose by listenin' to the stranger."

Everyone concentrated on Edge now.

"Get me a drink, Conrad," he said. "Take care of one of my needs. Whiskey."

"I'll get it," Fay Reeves called.

She rose into sight at one end of the long, copper-topped bar counter.

"Anything you don't do around this place?" Edge asked.

She came out from behind the bar with a full and uncorked bottle and a shot glass. "Plenty, feller," she replied as she set them down on the table and moved back to where she had been. "But it's not me people are interested in right now."

"It ain't often I see eye to eye with Fay," Stanton said as Edge poured himself a drink and knocked it back in one. He refilled the glass. "Speak your piece, stranger. I'm the sheriff. Jethro Lovejoy's the mayor and Maggie Woodward's the town treasurer—for a couple more days they are, anyway. That's an important audience in Democracy."

"And who the hell are you?" Nugent snarled, still scowling and squinting.

"Nobody important. Except to me."

"A killer, for one thing!" Forman growled. "He already admitted that, Gene."

"You certainly implied that, sir," the plump Maggie Woodward muttered.

Edge sipped the whiskey, set the glass down, and nodded. "In self-defense, ma'am. The reason I came to

45

town. So there'd be no misunderstanding about that point."

"Who?" Lovejoy asked nervously.

"Couple of fellers with badges," the half-breed supplied evenly and saw the anger deepen on the faces of Nugent and Forman as Stanton drew in a sharp breath. "Hogan and Danvers."

"You what?" Nugent rasped.

"Sonofabitch!" Forman croaked. "Arnie and Luke!"

Conrad broadened his grin as Lovejoy and Maggie Woodward were jolted by shock.

"Just your word that I shouldn't hang you, stranger?" Stanton said flatly. "A deputy named Robarts was ridin' with Hogan and Danvers. He still around to prove you ain't lyin'?"

Another sip of whiskey, accompanied by a shake of the head. "He got his first, feller. I figured to give him some pain for killing my horse. Dan Warren got in his shot first. He's good with a rifle. Or lucky."

There was life in the green eyes again. A dull light of interest. "They caught up with the Warrens?"

Conrad was suddenly sad. The two deputies continued to suffer the anger of frustration. The mayor and town treasurer were again rocked by shock. Fay Reeves listened with indifference.

Edge finished the second shot of whiskey and eased the bottle away from him. Then he explained what had happened at the derelict way station. He told the story dispassionately. Just the bare facts. He did not lie, or even bend the truth. He even told precisely how he had tricked Hogan and Danvers into having guns in their hands when he shot them.

"That's it, feller," he concluded.

"Crazy, like I said," the whore muttered.

Stanton's eyes were dead again. They had been since

the half-breed revealed that Dan and Laura Warren escaped unscathed from the gun battle at the way station. He grunted with dissatisfaction and waved irritably at the woman to be quiet. Then his lips folded back to display the false dentures in a sneer.

"Nice try, stranger. But I ain't buyin' your innocence just on account you rode into town on the horse of a man you murdered. I figure there's more to it than that."

"Damn right," Forman agreed.

"Weren't no call for him to blast Luke and Arnie that way," Nugent added.

"It certainly appears to have been wanton killing, Jethro," Maggie Woodward said shrilly as the elderly mayor continued to stare at Edge in horror.

Then Lovejoy gulped and nodded. "I agree," he said throatily. "We're sorry we attempted to interfere, Sheriff. You may be assured you have the backing of the present administration in dealing with this . . . this trigger-happy . . ."

"What d'you suggest, Mr. Mayor?" Stanton growled sardonically. "That I ask him nicely to surrender his guns and walk down to the jailhouse with me?"

"For the record," Edge said, "the answer to that question is no. Had my drink. Said what I came here to say. Intend to take a bath now. Then bed down. Kill anyone who tries to stop me."

He reached across to pick up the Winchester with his left hand and then got to his feet. His chair toppled over backwards.

"Cool as they come," Conrad said in a loud whisper, moving away from the wall beside the entrance.

Edge canted the rifle to his shoulder and dropped his right hand from the revolver butt. As he went around one side of the table, the Negro approached from the other side.

47

"I still ain't buyin' it!" Stanton snarled. "Not with seventy-five thousand of town money missin'."

"And Arnie, Luke, and Ed dead!" Nugent reminded forcefully.

Conrad picked up the bottle and glass and took them to the bar. He went around behind the counter to place them out of sight beneath it. The whore moved away from him, still seeming totally indifferent to what was happening.

"That's how many adds up to three, feller," Edge told the squint-eyed lawman as he stepped out of the saloon and into the lobby.

His back was towards the whole group and he sensed their eyes staring at him. His requirements as he had outlined them were simple. But it was not going to be easy to meet them. Or, if it was, the deferred price would be high.

But he had already committed himself to a course of action and had completed what he set out to do thus far. The same fate which had caused Dan Warren to take a shot at him had a free hand again. The man called Edge was ready to select from whichever new courses of action were offered him.

"Hold it, you murderin' bastard!" Forman barked. "Or get it in the back!"

Edge was midway across the lobby, angling towards the foot of the stairway. He halted and brought his trailing foot up alongside the other one.

"Don't kill him!" Jethro Lovejoy squealed. "He has to go on trial!"

"Hangin's the right way!" Stanton agreed, the legs of his chair scraping on the floor as he pushed it back and powered upright.

"Drop the rifle, deputy killer!" Nugent ordered.

Edge glanced back over his shoulder, turning only slightly from the waist.

Forman was still in a crouch, thrusting out at full arm's stretch the little .22 Smith and Wesson he had drawn from inside his boot. Stanton was immediately behind him, displaying a smile that was only a shade different from his customary sneer. Nugent was advancing fast into the lobby, moving in a half circle to give Edge a wide berth on his way to the stairs. Both deputies glowered hatred at the half-breed. Lovejoy and Maggie Woodward showed just their heads around the doorframe: and trembled at the prospect of violence at close quarters. The section of bar where Conrad and Fay Reeves had been standing was outside Edge's field of vision.

The half-breed unfisted his left hand and the Winchester slipped through and clattered to the wooden floor.

"Now the gunbelt!" Forman ordered.

He started to straighten and his partner broke into a short run for the foot of the stairs.

Edge moved both hands to the buckle of his belt. There was a strange expression of weary sadness on his lean, bristled face. It had been in place since he stepped out of the saloon: and did not alter by a single line as he powered into a whirling turn.

"Get him!" Stanton yelled.

Edge swung out his right foot: and his right hand moved to the butt of the Colt in a blur of speed.

Maggie Woodward screamed and was jerked into cover by Lovejoy.

The swinging foot hooked around a leg of the chair with the palette on it. Forman cursed and fired his small revolver. The crack of its report was almost masked by the thud of Edge's shoulder and hip against the floor.

Nugent froze for an instant at the foot of the stairs as

49

the bullet whined over Edge's falling form and exploded splinters from the banister rail.

Forman cocked his gun, but wasted a vital second in sidestepping to avoid the chair tumbling toward him.

Edge fired from the hip and rolled over on to his back.

Forman announced his death with a gurgling sound. Then fell to his knees with just a small bloody hole in his throat. But there was massive bleeding from his severed jugular vein. The bullet remained lodged in his windpipe for a moment, but the power of his final exhalation was too forceful. He spat out the bullet as he toppled forward. In its wake came a great gush of bright crimson that inscribed a two-yard-long splash on the floor in front of him.

Nugent was moving again—taking the stairs two at a time. Then he threw himself full-length to the steps, a hand far out ahead to reach for one of the discarded Colts.

Edge had to move his arm to adjust his aim.

Maggie Woodward started to scream—a long, strident, shrill sound on one constant note.

The half-breed's elbow was in a pool of green oil paint spilled from the palette. As he turned his arm to draw a bead on the squint-eyed deputy, his elbow slithered in the wrong direction. His expression changed then, his eyes narrowing to glittering threads, his nostrils flaring, and his lips pulling back to form his mouth into an animal snarl.

But the hatred which emanated from the contorted features with a seemingly palpable force was not directed at Nugent. Even though the deputy had scooped up a revolver, cocked it, and thrust it between the banister rails.

For Nugent was just the instrument of the violent death that had always been inevitable. It could have

50

been any finger curled around the trigger and taking first pressure to blast a .45 bullet into the body of Edge.

Frank Forrest had never done it. Nor Hal Douglas, Bob Rhett . . . John Scott . . . Billy Seward. During the war or after it. Nor any one of many Indians. Nor a Mexican bandit called El Matador. Nor Jonas Pike, who considered he should have married Beth instead of Edge. Nor any one of countless men and several women who had had good reason to be the instrument of his death in the violent past.

For fate had selected a man named Nugent. And had decided that the place of his death should be the lobby of the Palace Hotel in a Nebraska town called Democracy.

But the half-breed did not simply submit to the inevitable. Although he knew he had no chance of getting his gun back to the aim before Nugent fired, he made the attempt.

And, just for an instant, he thought the explosion that sounded in his ears was some dreadful portent of eternal damnation. But this momentary lapse into the useless abstract of imagination was corrected by the awesome evidence of his eyes.

It was the deputy on the stairway who was dead. A jagged hole had been blasted in the banister rails and through this could be seen the mutilated remains of what once had been a man. From the waist down he was still in recognizable human form. But his torso and head were a crimson, featureless parody of what had existed a moment ago. At the instant of impact, the deputy was lifted and slammed against the wall. He seemed to remain there for a long time, frozen into immobility. Then the sheened covering of blood flowed. And shiny white bone could be seen. The skull with its eye sockets and the tobacco browned teeth. The rib cage and hip bones. The heart was revealed then, to be a darker

51

shade of red than the tissue around it. The bunched intestines were a yellowish color. There was a ragged hole in the stomach and half-digested food ran out, looking like vomit.

Time was warped, for all this was seen in only part of a second: before gravity forced the shattered corpse to tip forward on to the stairway then slide down, leaving a slimy crimson train on the plush carpet.

A hand cracked against flesh and the shrill screaming was curtailed.

Edge powered to his haunches and then came erect, whirling to track the Colt towards the saloon entrance. But death had paid its grim visit and left.

Mayor Lovejoy was sagging against the doorframe, his once ruddy complexion the color of dirty snow. Fay Reeves was backing away from Maggie Woodward, the younger woman as indifferent as before while the older one glared angrily at her and rubbed the side of her jaw.

"You'll hang, stranger," Sheriff Stanton croaked, absently wiping the clean paintbrush with a soiled rag as his dead eyes watched the half-breed holster the Colt. "For murderin' a peace officer in the act of resistin' arrest. Three counts. Forman here in town and Hogan and Danvers out at the way station."

"Mrs. Woodward and me saw it with our own eyes," Lovejoy rasped. "It was the most cold-blooded, disgusting ..."

The older woman forgot her pain and the whore to nod her agreement as the mayor's voice trailed away.

"And you'll swing for committin' the same crime, Power!" Stanton went on, hurling away the brush and rag as he snapped his head around to fix the Negro with an unemotional stare. "One count. Nugent, while aidin' and abettin'."

Conrad Power was grinning as he broke open the double-barreled shotgun and used a thumbnail to eject two spent cartridges. Acrid-smelling smoke curled out of both breeches. "I hear you talkin' to me, but I don't see you doin' nothin' about it, gent."

"Because he's fresh out of helpers, the bastard!" Fay Reeves spat.

Edge retrieved his Winchester, went to the foot of the stairs, and stepped across the crumpled remains of Nugent.

"Edge!" the wan-faced mayor called shrilly, and the half-breed came to a halt, close to the top of the stairs.

"You want something?"

Lovejoy was frightened by the weary tone of voice and the total lack of expression on the bristled face—the complete indifference of a man who had escaped death by a split-second and been responsible for the violent endings of two other lives. No more than half a minute ago.

"Whatever Conrad Power told you, he was speaking as an individual. The present administration of this town will never condone the use of violence to achieve its aims."

"Didn't tell him nothin', Mr. Lovejoy," the Negro supplied, still grinning. "Exceptin' that the gent here don't never say nothin' he don't intend to do."

Stanton moved out of the saloon and into the lobby. Whatever emotions he was experiencing behind his dead eyes took the easygoing attitude out of his gait and he walked on stiff legs, his body held woodenly erect. "Call a meetin', Lovejoy!" he ordered. "Fine words don't do nothin' to keep our town clean of filth!"

He shot a final glance towards Edge before he wrenched open the double doors and marched out.

"Come, my dear," Lovejoy urged, taking Mrs. Woodward's trembling arm. "We never thought we would see the day, I know—but necessity makes for strange bedfellows."

He steered her carefully around the slumped corpse of Forman and made sure he blocked the shattered body of Nugent from her view. The double doors remained open after the couple had gone out into the cold night. Fresh, damp air continued to stream in, neutralizing the final remnants of gunsmoke.

"I got the same aims as the mayor and them that back him, Mr. Edge," Conrad Power said, replacing the grin with an expression of grim determination. "But in a dirty fight a man that only punches clean is just bound to lose. Wouldn't you say that?"

"I'd say you aim high, feller," the half-breed answered, with a dispassionate glance down at the dead Nugent—just a pair of obviously human legs splayed out from a heap of blood-soaked pulp. "Two hits and both above the belt."

Chapter Five

FROM the windows of room seven, Edge could see several lights gleaming in the darkness. And a number of people were moving on the streets, heading for a building sited on the northeast corner of the intersection. He spent only a moment looking at the scene, illuminated by a brightening moon that was fast beginning to dominate a star-sprinkled sky as the clouds fled into the east. Then he used a blanket from the bed to drape the smashed window and turned to watch Fay Reeves come into the room, a pail of steaming water in each hand.

"Conrad's gone to get Amos Meek to take the corpses away," she announced. "He says you can move to another room if you want."

"Trouble enough in Democracy," he told her. "I wouldn't want to put anybody to any more. This room's fine."

She righted the tub from where it had been kicked over by the deputy and emptied the pails into it. Then she went out, leaving the door open. Edge waited until she had made two more trips and the tub was half full before he stripped off his clothes. The town streets were deserted again by then, all those who had been roused from their beds now assembled in the town meeting hall on the opposite corner of the intersection.

He had used a bar of soap to lather himself by the

time the whore returned with two final pails of water and a towel. She appraised his lean, hard body with a coldly professional look as he lowered himself into the tub and she tipped the new water over him.

"This and the others . . ." she said, trailing gentle fingers over the scar tissue on his left shoulder. ". . . from times when there wasn't anyone like Conrad around."

The other wounds she had seen were on his hip, thigh, and arm. Most were indelible relics of the war. The most recent—a livid, puckered groove in his left arm—was the result of a life-or-death gunfight on the burning sands of a Nevada desert just a few short weeks ago.

"Didn't ask him to blast the deputy, ma'am," Edge answered, as he lathered his face and drew the razor from the neck pouch.

"If he didn't, you'd be dead." She backed away from him to stand by the undraped window. "Don't you care about that, feller?"

Edge removed the long bristles with smooth, rasping strokes of the razor. Another relic of wartime, more useful than the desultory conversation pieces of his wounds.

"Yeah, I care. Because it means I owe him."

She shook her head without looking at him. "He doesn't think of it as a debt, feller. Maybe he even thinks that he owes you. Because you gave him an excuse to hit back at that bastard Stanton."

Edge continued to shave, hearing movement in the lobby below. Footfalls on the polished floor, low-voiced talk, and dragging sounds. He guessed that the town mortician had come to collect the bodies.

"The sheriff's pride was hurt, that's all."

"Sure was!" the whore muttered in a tone of grim satisfaction. "And he's one proud bastard. Kill a man and he don't feel anythin' any more. It's the livin' that suffer, you know what I mean?"

"For a while," Edge answered as he finished shaving

56

and reached for one of his boots. He stropped the razor on its leather to hone the dulled blade.

Down below, the talk ended and the double doors banged close. Footfalls marked the progress of a man up the stairway.

"A while could be long enough to get Stanton and his crowd off Democracy's back, feller." She sighed. "Then again, maybe you and Conrad'll get hung and nothin' won't be changed. Meek's headin' for the meetin'."

"All the big wheels are over there," Power said from the doorway of the room. "But I reckon we can count on Sam Flint and Jody Tillson not backing the gent."

The Negro still had the shotgun. As he leaned against the doorframe he fed fresh cartridges into the breeches and snapped the weapon closed.

"This feller figures he owes you for savin' his life, Conrad," the whore said, turning her back on the window to watch as Edge stepped from the tub and began to towel himself dry.

Power gave a dismissing wave of his hand. "Ain't nobody owes nobody nothin'. I guess a man like you got payment in advance from Dan Warren, uh?"

"Guess again, feller."

The Negro blinked. "Then I don't get it, mister. Why'd you kill them deputies out at the way station, then come into town to rile up the gent?"

"Maybe he's just a natural-born troublemaker, Conrad," Fay Reeves suggested flatly. "He sure enough kills without turnin' a hair."

Edge had pulled on his red underwear and now sat on the bed to don his pants and shirt. "Don't make it," he corrected evenly. "Find it or it finds me."

"You mean you don't know what's happenin' in this town?" Power asked, startled.

Edge put on his boots and buckled the gunbelt about his waist. Then he leaned the Winchester against the bed and spread himself out on top of the covers. "I figure you'll tell me, feller. At the drop of a hat."

He reached for his hat on one of the chairs and placed it over his face.

"He's ready to listen," the whore said.

"Watch the town hall," Power snapped, and stepped across the threshold, swinging the door closed behind him.

The draught which billowed the blanket at the window was abruptly stopped. But it was still very cold in the room.

"This used to be a nice, smooth-runnin' town, mister," the Negro began. "More or less owned by Louis Warren, Dan's old man. I was born and raised here, like most other folk in Democracy today. It was always a good place to live in. Until Louis Warren died of the old age and a few folks started to stir the shit. Frank Snyder did most of the stirrin'. And he found plenty of help to push the bill of goods he was sellin'.

"You listenin' to me, mister?"

"I owe you," Edge muttered into the darkness of his hat. "Listening to hear the size of the debt."

"Have it your way."

"Usually do, feller."

The whore spat. Edge heard the globule of moisture hit the floor, but there was no sound of her shoe spreading the wet.

"Snyder's the owner of the local dry goods business here in town," Power went on. "Always has been a fancy talker. Him and Amos Meek, the mortician, Harry Grant and Silas McQuigg who run the livery and blacksmith and Jay Bailey, the barber, they been poker-playin' buddies from way back. Soon as old Louis Warren kicked the bucket, they didn't play much poker any more. Had Stanton and Larry Swan to join their group at the corner

58

table in the hotel saloon every night. Swan's the banker here in Democracy, did I tell you that?"

"You did now."

"Anyway, it was talk they'd get together for. Snyder did most of it at first. But, pretty soon, they was all havin' their pieces to say. Exceptin' for Stanton. He ain't never been one much for words."

"Maybe they should have invited you instead of the sheriff," Edge said wryly.

"All right, I'm gettin' to the point, mister," Power growled peevishly. "Just fillin' you in on the background. Upshot of all this talkin' was that Frank Snyder and the others decided to run against the town council at the next election. First time it's ever been done. Only time before anyone new got on the council was when one of the councillors died."

"How'd this town get to be called Democracy?" Edge asked rhetorically.

There was a roar in the meeting hall across the intersection, muted by walls and distance. Then the group became quiet again.

"Louis Warren called it that when he built it," Power answered quickly. "First he staked out claim to his range and then he started the town. Left it up to the folks who came how they wanted to run the place. And the folks elected the town council without making no plans to change it. And, like I told you, it ran smooth and nice up until old man Warren died. Folks minded their own business and Stanton had the easiest job in the whole U S of A. On account of there was never no trouble here."

"You've probably seen his lousy paintin's spread all over town, feller," Fay Reeves muttered. "All he had to fill his time with."

"Made an art out of doing nothing, uh?" the half-breed said.

"Seems like he was just bidin' his time, waitin' for

59

somethin' to happen," the Negro supplied. "And somethin' sure happened when Snyder and his buddies put it around that Dan Warren and his wife didn't have no right to take over where old Louis left off." He paused. "You sure that Warren didn't tell you none of this, mister?"

"Was too busy—protecting his good name and staying alive."

"This feller don't need tellin' anythin' twice, Conrad," the whore reminded. "I reckon the meetin'll be over pretty soon."

"Frig the meetin'," Power rasped. "Won't none of them fancy talkers tangle with us. They'll wait for the gent to bring in guns in place of them that's dead. That's what the meetin's for. That's the point of it."

"Taking as long to get to it as you are, feller," the half-breed prompted.

"Sure. Sure. All right. Election time was comin' up. Same as it does every four years. In the past, was always done on a show of hands. Whole town gathered in the square outside the hotel. Old Louis Warren was always around. Asked if folks wanted the same council as before. Everyone put up his hand. Then came into the saloon to drink free—old man Warren pickin' up the tab. All nice and smooth. But this time, Snyder and his bunch put it around they was goin' to stand against Lovejoy and the others on the council. And they made lots of promises about what they was goin' to do when they got elected."

"That bastard Stanton's left the meetin'," the whore reported from the window. "Looks like he's goin' ... yeah, he's headed for the telegraph office."

"Folks laughed in their faces at first," Power hurried on. "But then they got to thinkin' and a lot of them reckoned Snyder was makin' good sense."

"Everyone's leavin'," Fay Reeves broke in. "Yeah, the

meetin's over. All goin' home, looks like. Tillson and Flint as well. Maybe you ain't got nobody except this feller, Conrad."

"Time'll tell," the Negro countered. "Anyway, mister, what won folks over was Snyder's promise to take the Big-B spread away from Dan Warren and sell sections of it to anyone who wanted them—dirt cheap. Larry Swan was gonna put up the cash for loans and give the interest to the town. And the town was gonna use the interest money to build a new school, a canning plant, an infirmary, and all things like that."

"And a new marker naming the town Utopia?" Edge muttered.

"What?"

"Utopia."

"I don't get it."

"So forget it. Nobody ever does."

"Folks liked what Snyder and his bunch were tellin' them. But they'd had a lot of respect for old man Warren and they didn't have no reason to want to screw his son. So Snyder changed his ideas around a bit. And he got Swan to back him in offerin' Dan seventy-five grand for the Big-B."

"Stanton's through at the telegraph office," Fay Reeves said dully. "Goin' back to his office. Everyone else is already bedded down again, looks like."

"Told you they wouldn't do nothin' tonight," Power reminded. "Crazy price for God knows how many acres of the only decent grazin' and farmin' land in Carroll County. And Dan told them he wasn't gonna sell at any price, anyways. Which was when Swan rode stage all the way across to the state capital at Lincoln and checked the records. Found out old man Warren never registered his claim to the Big-B."

Power's voice suddenly took on a strange tone of vehement sadness. "And folks that had always believed a man could pay for what was his in sweat and toil figured they could change their mind. Didn't do nothin' to help either way. Just stood by and watched while the Snyder bunch took Stanton's hired guns out to the Big-B and run off Dan and Laura Warren. Then got drunk downstairs. Free. With Frank Snyder pickin' up the tab this time."

"So you needn't get no sleepless nights about killin' the deputies, feller," the whore muttered. "Not that you would, I figure. But they were all nothin' but fast guns for hire until that bastard Stanton brought them to Democracy and gave them badges." Then she vented a short, harsh laugh. "Same as you, I guess. Only you ain't hired and you ain't got a badge."

"Shut your mouth, Fay," Power said flatly, without rancor. "Pay no attention to her, Edge."

"I'm paying nothing to her, feller," the half-breed answered. "Which is why she doesn't like me, I figure."

"I'm almost through," Power hurried on, as the whore scowled and seemed about to snap an angry retort. "Dan and Laura moved into the Palace and did their best to stir up folks against the Snyder bunch. But weren't hardly anybody would listen. On account of most were too busy gettin' money from the bank and fencin' off their sections of the Big-B."

"Who else listened, feller—apart from you and the whore?"

"Count me out, feller!" Fay Reeves snapped. "I told you already, I'm neutral."

"The schoolteacher, Tillson. And the Reverend Flint," the Negro answered, glowering at the sullen-faced woman. "They figured the same as the Warrens and me. Snyder and his bunch ain't in this for nothin' 'ceptin' their own good. If they're let alone to get what they want, won't be anyone in Democracy and the whole of Carroll County who ain't in hock to this town for their mortgage. That time comes, the Snyder bunch'll be rulers of the whole friggin' roost. And that time'll be a hell of a lot nearer if Snyder and his crowd win the election day after tomorrow."

The black man sighed ruefully. "I sure thought you was workin' for the Warrens when you came to town, mister."

"Just didn't want to be wanted, feller—especially by the law. Your mistake. Everyone makes them from time to time."

"Even you?" Fay Reeves growled.

"No one's perfect, lady. Same as no one can take on a whole town if everybody else in it is set on doing what they want to do. No two people. Or even four, if the schoolteacher and the padre are willing to do more than attend meetings."

He raised the brim of his hat to look through the cold and moonlit air of the room at Power. The black man was leaning his back against the door, gripping the shotgun tightly in both hands. An angry frown appeared suddenly on the handsome face of the young Negro.

"What the hell you figure the Warrens plan to do, mister?" he snarled. "Just take the money and run? Well, they don't! I helped them bust into the bank last night. And I was for them takin' every cent. But they wouldn't. Just the seventy-five grand they was offered for their place. And they're gonna use that money to get help." The anger drained out of him and disappointment was spread across his face in its place. "Man, I really thought you was the first of it. That's what I told the mayor and Maggie Woodward. And they was all fired up because of what I told them. Same as a lot of other folks'll be ready to make a stand against the Snyder bunch if they got backin'."

"Which other folks?" Edge posed, hiding his face with his hat again.

"Them that ain't got no interest in claim jumpin', mister. Storekeepers and merchants. Folks like me who own places here in town. Started them up themselves or took over them when their parents died. They can see—a lot of them—that the Snyder bunch won't stop at taking the Big-B range. When they got that all sewn up, they'll start in on property here in Democracy. But they're too scared to do anythin' about it right now. Same as the Snyder bunch was too scared before Stanton brought in them gunslingers and deputized them."

"Same as Conrad's scared now," the whore said lightly.

"Shut your mouth!" the Negro snarled, and there was viciousness in his tone now.

"What'll you do if I won't?" she countered in the same tone. "You and everyone else in this stinkin' town make me sick to my stomach. All of you talk up a storm, but ain't none of you make a move until you got some stranger's muscle to hide behind. And what d'you do when the muscle's dead or won't help you no more? Go back to bein' the yellow jellies you was before the muscle showed up, that's what!"

Her heels rapped rapidly against the floor, counterpointing the rustle of her gown, as she flounced across the room. She wrenched open the door and glared back towards the half-breed stretched out on the bed.

"So maybe you can see why I'm neutral, feller!" she snapped. "Some choice, uh? Lovejoy's spineless lot or Snyder's bunch of lily-livered crooks. All of them needin' somebody else's strong arm and fast gun to back them. It won't make no difference who wins the lousy election."

"Yeah, I see," Edge drawled wryly. "You being what you are."

"What's that got to do with it?" Fay Reeves demanded.

Edge raised his hat, just high enough to display his teeth, gleaming in a moonlit grin. "A whore don't care who gets in."

Chapter Six

CONRAD Power asked one question, his tone anxious. He received an affirmative reply that sent him out of the room with a smile, only a few moments after Fay Reeves had left. Edge got under the bed covers then and slept. It was a sound sleep which, as the whore had predicted, was untroubled by pangs of conscience about the men he had killed.

Perhaps none of them would have killed the half-breed, but all had threatened his freedom of movement: which did not amount to the same thing, but came close. The fact that they were doing their duty as lawmen was immaterial. Thus, by the same token, it made no difference to Edge's attitude that they were not peace officers by vocation or profession: instead were gunslingers imported to Democracy and given badges to handle a specific situation.

None of these thoughts ran through his sleeping mind. Throughout the night and the lightening early hours which heralded the dawning of a new day, Edge rested undisturbed. He did not sleep deeply—never had done since the first days of the shooting war when he had learned that a split-second delay in coming awake could make the difference between life and death. He slept like a wild animal, restocking his physical energy and replenishing whatever the previous day had drained

66

from his mental faculties. While, all in time, his mind was held just below the level of awareness and his muscular reflexes remained in a state of readiness.

The least hint of danger would spring him awake: his right hand was poised to reach for Winchester, Colt, or razor.

Reflected sunlight roused him, glinting yellow as it was bounced off glass across the intersection and directed into the room through the unbroken window. As he rose from the bed and crossed to take down the blanket from the shattered window, the town clock chimed six times.

The air he breathed in was as chill as it had been the night before. But the smoke which tainted its freshness came from woodfires rather than exploded bullets. It rose from a host of chimneys, pointing up at a cloudless, light blue sky like so many solid black fingers. It was allowed to rise very high through the stillness before air currents disintegrated it.

He leaned far out of the window then, to survey the town. Democracy was awake, but the many cooking and heating fires were the sole signs that it was stirring. In this early morning, it looked like the kind of nice, easy-to-live-in town which the Negro had said it used to be. A town of substantially built houses and business premises with no fancy trimmings. It was sited on a high plain of mostly lush grass country. Far to the west the horizon was marked by a line of jagged peaks. In the other directions Edge could see from the window—the east and the north from where he had come—there were just gently rolling hills stretching into seeming infinity, featured here and there by rock outcrops, bluffs, water courses, and stands of timber.

Among these natural formations on the vast landscape, fashioned over hundreds, thousands, and even millions of years, were the much more recent man-made scars that were the reasons for trouble in Democracy. The fence poles, some already strung with wire, the parked wagons loaded with timber, and the half-built shacks that showed the Big-B range was well advanced towards the reformation Snyder had promised.

Much closer to where the half-breed stood at the hotel window, reflecting coolly on his actions of the night before, were the canvas banners spanning the broad streets. They were painted garishly with slogans exhorting the local citizens to vote for the platform which had scored a victory before attaining office. *FRANK (AND HONEST) SNYDER does not make idle promises! Vote MEEK for a better life. HARRY GRANT and SILAS McQUIGG make horsesense. You can bank on LARRY SWAN. JAY BAILEY can cut taxes as well as hair!*

As the ice blue eyes, narrowed against the strengthening sunlight, scanned the banners—failing to spot any counterclaims on behalf of the present town councillors—he saw a movement on the east section of the cross street. The door of Grant's Livery Stable was swung wide and he recognised the warmly clad figure of Fay Reeves as the whore led a big, strong-looking black stallion on to the street. She mounted hurriedly, her knees banging against bulging saddlebags. About to heel the animal forward, she hesitated, and looked fearfully around. She spotted Edge at the broken window and it took her a long time to force a smile to her face, which this morning was cleaned of paint and looked haggard and old. Then she raised a hand in farewell and slammed her heels against the stallion's flanks to lunge the animal into a fast gallop, heading east. The hooves of the horse sounded loud on the frost-hardened mud of the street.

Knuckles rapped on the door as it was pushed open.

"Only me," Power announced. "Fay's leavin' town, Edge."

"Maybe absence will make the heart grow fonder," the half-breed muttered, turning from the window.

The Negro did not look so black today. His eyes were bloodshot from lack of sleep and his too-tight clothes were rumpled. The double-barreled shotgun seemed to be a part of him.

"She spent the night with Clarence Engle in his room behind the telegraph office," Power added nervously. "You figure she found out somethin' we don't know? Maybe about the message Stanton sent last night after the meetin'?"

"Sure didn't get bored along with bed," Edge allowed, picking up his long topcoat as he crossed the room.

He left the Winchester and the rest of his gear and Power showed a wan grin.

"I sure am glad you're still around, Edge."

"It shows, feller."

Last night, just before he left the room, the Negro had asked the half-breed to stay in town until the Warrens brought help. Edge's affirmative answer had been: *"I owe you."*

Now Edge led the way down into the lobby. Blood, dried dark brown, stained the carpet on the lower stairs, the wall, and the threshold of the saloon. Much brighter staining showed on the floor in the center of the lobby, where the multicolored paints had been spilled from Stanton's palette. The half-breed followed his nose, tracking the smell of coffee into the saloon.

Power had spent the night in here, sitting in a chair at a table positioned so he could see every window, the closed doors which gave access from the street and the entrance from the lobby. He had smoked a lot, the stubs of cigarettes littering the floor around the chair. And, unless there had been a first bottle, had drunk sparingly from a bottle of rye whiskey.

"Coffee's on," the black man said, his mood brightening by the moment as he went behind the bar counter. "Fix ham and eggs if you're hungry."

"Just coffee," Edge told him.

"Comin' right up," Power called, after ducking through an archway hung with a beaded curtain.

Edge sat in a chair across the table from the one Power had used and a few moments later the Negro reappeared, carrying a coffee pot and two tin mugs. He tried to keep the grin in place as he sat down and poured the coffee, but he lost the battle.

"Fay was right," he said at length, his tone melancholic. "Ain't no one in this town with any backbone worth a damn. Me included. I spent the whole lousy night shakin' in my shoes about what I did." The shotgun was on the table and he touched it lightly, almost fearfully. "One minute I'm holdin' still for Stanton to paint my picture. Next I'm blastin' Nugent to bits. And enjoyin' it. About the only good thing can be said for me is that I ain't blamin' you for what I done."

Edge sipped his coffee and Power swallowed hard without touching his.

"I don't like Fay leavin' the way she did, Edge," the Negro hurried on, licking his lips. "She's been whorin' here at the Palace since the time when my Pa ran it. And I ain't never seen her scared of nothin' before. But somethin' sure set her runnin' scared this mornin'."

"Who's Engle rooting for?" Edge asked.

The Negro grimaced. "He's got himself a prime piece of the old Big-B. Had enough of tappin' that key down at the telegraph office."

"Where's the wire go?"

"Closest place is Laramie over to the northwest. South to Cheyenne. Hogan and Nugent and the others came in from Laramie. Just a day's ride away. Or a night's."

His bloodshot eyes moved to rake along the windows. Through them there was nothing to see except the

70

empty street and the façades of the buildings on the other side.

Edge finished the coffee, nodded, and stood up.

"Where you goin'?" Fast and anxious.

"Get a horse, feller."

"You ain't leavin'?"

"Told you, I owe you. Anyplace in town that sells horses?"

"Harry Grant trades down at his livery. But he won't be overanxious to do business with you, Edge."

"Then that'll be his problem," the half-breed answered as he headed across to the doorway which gave directly on to the street.

He put on the thick, calf-length coat before he shot the bolts on the main door, swung it open, and pushed through the batswings. The sun was completely clear of the eastern horizon now, but did not deliver on the warmth promised by its brightness. Edge did not button the coat as he stepped down from the sidewalk and crossed the intersection. The smell of woodsmoke was now mixed in with the aromas of boiling coffee and cooking food.

As he moved along the north sidewalk of the east section of cross street, he glanced at the signboards above the solidly shut doorways of the business premises. Young's Drugstore, next to the town meeting hall; Bailey's Haircuts and Shaves; *Democracy Clarion*—editor and proprietor Thomas C. Waters; Margaret's Millinery. Then the sidewalk ran out short of the big double doors at the front of the livery stable and the blacksmith's forge beyond.

Somebody had closed the stable doors after the whore had taken out the stallion. As Edge creaked open one of them, a man with a gravel voice said:

"You come to steal another horse, mister?"

"You figure to kill us?" another man, with a reedy

71

voice added. "Same as you did Hogan to get his geldin'?"

The gravel-voiced one wore a leather blacksmith's apron, which probably meant he was Silas McQuigg. Edge guessed the other man was Harry Grant. He was dressed in faded brown dungarees.

"You fellers are up early," Edge replied as he stepped into the rich-smelling stable.

"We got a business to run," McQuigg croaked. He was short, but powerfully built with big, calloused hands and a round, sour-looking face. In his late forties.

"Always plenty to do around here," Grant said. He was in the same age group as his partner. Tall and thin, with a small beard, neatly trimmed. It grew grey although the hair on his head was jet black. There was a crafty look in his brown eyes.

Edge glanced around the neatly kept stable with its dozen stalls, ten of which were occupied. He wrinkled his nose against the smell of horse-wet straw and fresh droppings. Then showed his teeth in a mild smile. "In a stable, work's always piling up, I guess."

McQuigg continued to look sour and Grant's eyes retained their crafty expression.

"Need a horse," Edge said into the uneasy silence, moving across the stable. The two men remained standing by the pot-bellied stove on which a coffee pot had not yet started to bubble. "Not that one. Solid color makes for a stronger animal."

He nodded towards the piebald which he had ridden in from the derelict way station last night.

"Ain't none for sale that ain't spoken for, mister," Grant answered.

McQuigg parted his lips in a thin, cruel smile. "Ain't exactly true, Harry. The bay mare you can have, mister. Thousand dollars."

Grant sucked in a fast breath.

72

McQuigg continued to smile as Edge glanced at him, saw the stall he indicated, then ambled across to it. But then his expression became sourer than before when the half-breed moved into the stall and began to examine the mare. The brown-skinned hands ran expertly over the flanks and legs, then the belly. He lifted the tail, then moved to look at the teeth and eyes of the horse. There was a rope bridle on the mare and he took hold of this to lead the animal from the stall.

"You drive a hard bargain, feller," Edge said lightly. "But you've got yourself a deal."

"Don't be crazy!" the blacksmith snarled, his flesh flushing with anger. "Even if you could afford a thousand bucks, you know there ain't a work horse around worth anywhere near that much."

Grant nodded vigorously.

The town clock started to chime seven. Between each ringing note the sounds of hooves and wagon wheels could be heard, reaching into town from out along the north trail.

"I know that, feller," Edge agreed. "And I guess Stanton's smart enough to know it, too."

Neither man was wearing a gunbelt. Fists clenched, McQuigg moved quickly from the stove to stand in the open doorway. Grant seemed about to follow him, then glanced at the half-breed and held back.

"Gene Stanton wouldn't give you the drippin's of his nose, mister!" the blacksmith growled. "You better put that nag back in the stall."

Edge sighed. "Officer of the county killed my horse. Fixed it up with another officer of the county that my horse would be replaced. Charged to the county. Be obliged if you'd step aside now, feller. And maybe go do some dickering with the sheriff."

The hoofbeats and rolling wheels sounded in town now, slower, but louder as the noise was echoed be-

73

tween building façades. Then they halted, somewhere close to the midtown intersection.

"Must be the eight o'clock stage from Laramie, Silas," Grant said, the reediness of his voice emphasized by his fear of the situation. "Almost an hour early."

"Seems like you're the one with business to do at the law office, mister," McQuigg muttered, advancing slowly on where Edge stood holding the rope bridle of the mare. "You get me and Harry cash on the line from Sheriff Stanton and then you can take the nag." The grin parted his lips again. "You know the askin' price."

"Silas, he's packin' a gun!" Grant warned.

There was an abrupt explosion of voices down near the intersection. Loud, but reaching the livery as no more than a babble as many men shouted at once.

Grant hurried across to the open doorway. McQuigg made to turn, as if to look at him for information. But he abruptly lunged at Edge, aiming his meaty shoulder to slam it into the half-breed's chest. He clasped his hands together into a tight, single fist. And swung both arms upwards.

The blacksmith's eyes had telegraphed the attack: had swiveled hard over in their sockets to keep Edge in view as he pretended an interest in Grant.

Edge sidestepped, away from the mare. The lunging shoulder of the blacksmith brushed his upper arm. And, as the half-breed snapped his head back, the double-handed fist clipped the front of his hat brim.

McQuigg's own momentum carried him fast between the suddenly nervous mare and the momentarily immobile Edge. Edge swung around to track after the blacksmith.

"I'll go get Gene!" Grant promised shrilly, and raced out of the livery.

McQuigg halted too early and was unbalanced. He was half-turned towards Edge when the half-breed

74

pushed out a hand. His palm cupped the fleshy cheek and required little pressure to send the powerfully built man to the straw-scattered ground. The impact gushed a stream of hot air and a groan out of the blacksmith's gaping mouth. Then:

"No!" he croaked, covering his face with his hands as Edge drew a straight razor from the neck pouch. The trembling fingers of the hands were splayed just enough so that McQuigg could see between them. It was too cold for the beads of moisture which squeezed through the fingers to be sweat. "Take the horse, please!"

"Intend to," Edge said evenly, dropping into a crouch beside the quaking man.

"Don't kill me, please!" He had lost his croaking tone and his voice was almost as shrill as that of Grant.

"Relax, feller. Who did Stanton send for after the meeting last night?"

"What?" McQuigg took his hands away from his face. His eyes, glistening with the tears of earlier terror, were wide and staring, fixed upon the blade of the razor as Edge used it to pare a fingernail.

"You ain't deaf, feller. If you want to act dumb, I can make it for real."

The razor continued to peel away slivers of nail. The flat tone of the half-breed drew the blacksmith's stare to his face. The basic lines of the expression were in calm repose. But the clear blue eyes, peering out through the narrowed lids, seemed to emanate the collective evil of the world.

"The Kerwins," McQuigg answered in a muted shriek. "And them that ride with them."

"Tough bunch, uh?"

"Ain't no gang of outlaws tougher, it's said. So best you take that mare and ride, mister."

"Power was wrong," Edge mused.

"What?" The big eyes blinked the man's confusion.

75

"At least one man in this town ready to fight for what's his."

McQuigg scowled. "And where did it get me against a man like you?"

"On the losing side, feller."

The hand holding the razor moved fast away from the free one: to the side and down. McQuigg groaned his terror as he saw the blade close to his eyes. Then attempted to push the back of his head into the dirt floor as his flesh was cut and blood spurted.

Just as Edge had experienced a foreboding of imminent death last night, so the blacksmith endured the same feelings now. But he closed his eyes. And did not open them to realize he was alive until he heard the half-breed cluck the mare into movement.

He saw the tall man and the big horse in dark silhouette against the sunlit street. He groaned his relief and pressed the palm of his hand to his forehead where two shallow cuts were beginning to sting, the slight pain stronger than the sensation of warm blood flowing from them.

As he folded up into a sitting posture, he brought the hand down in front of his face. Printed in slick crimson on his palm was a large X.

"Why did you do that?" he called out through the doorway to Edge, his voice deep and harsh again.

"Don't know much about politics and elections," the half-breed answered. "But any man willing to make a stand gets my vote."

Chapter Seven

THE depot of the Wyoming-Nebraska-Colorado Stage Line was on the northwest corner of the intersection. As Edge led the big mare along the cross street, taking note of the smooth and easy way she walked and how she held her head high, he saw that Grant had been right about the stage arriving early.

The battered Concord with four weary-looking and travel-stained horses in the traces was parked outside the depot. Disembarked passengers were inside the depot, looking out through the doorway and windows as three canvas-shrouded bodies were off-loaded from the roof of the coach. They were being transferred to a glass-sided hearse with the legend A. MEEK TASTE-FUL FUNERALS painted under the glass panels in flowing script.

Across the intersection, another vehicle was parked, outside the angled entrance of the hotel. This was a buckboard drawn by just a pair of horses. Up on the seat sat a short, very fat man dressed in a frock coat and high hat. He was the main center of attention, for the buckboard was surrounded by a large group of people, many of them talking to him at once. He was confused and angry: until Sheriff Stanton broke from the group and started across the intersection. Harry Grant trailed the lawman for a few yards, but then drew back. All eyes swung towards Stanton, then raked along the street to locate the advancing half-breed. Even the chore of off-loading the shrouded corpses from the stage to the hearse was interrupted.

"You're just plain, friggin' mean!" the injured McQuigg snarled as he emerged from the livery, mopping at his bloodied forehead with a kerchief. "You didn't have to mark me this way! I was down and finished."

Edge did not look back as he moved slowly towards Stanton, who had halted at the center of the intersection. "You're still alive, feller," he answered, just loud enough for the blacksmith to hear him. "Tried to stop me getting what I was owed. Anyone asks you why you got that mark, you tell them that. Kind of a warning to all. Oh yeah, you can also spread it around I got this thing about having a gun aimed at me."

Stanton was not wearing a topcoat against the bright cold of the morning. He was dressed in his neat city suit, but the tailored line of his jacket was spoiled by the gunbelt and holster he wore today. As Edge reached the end of the cross street, the lawman unbuttoned the jacket and hooked the thumb of his right hand over the front of the gunbelt, so that his palm was only six inches from the ivory butt of a well-kept Beaumont-Adams .45.

"What's wrong with Silas McQuigg, stranger?" Stanton demanded, his eyes looking deader and greener than ever as he surveyed the half-breed with the icy calmness of a skilled gunfighter.

The two separate groups of watchers behind him to left and right seemed to be holding their breath.

In contrast to the sheriff's ramrod-stiff stance, Edge appeared negligently nonchalant as he held the rope bridle in his left hand and allowed his right to hang limply at his side. He pursed his lips and turned his head unhurriedly to look back along the street at the blacksmith. McQuigg was still standing outside the livery doorway, tentatively dabbing at his cut forehead.

"Thinks he's hard done by," the half-breed answered, returning his apparently arrogantly indifferent attention to Stanton. "Feeling a little cross.".

"You okay, Silas?" Grant yelled.

"On top of the friggin' world!" the blacksmith bellowed with heavy sarcasm. "You watch that sneaky bastard, Gene!"

He whirled and stormed back into the livery.

"He's right, Gene," the fat man on the buckboard called. "A dead hero is no use for the cause we're fighting for."

"Don't call him, Gene," the man supervising the handling of the corpses warned. "Not when you've got help coming."

Meek was attired suitably for his profession. His boots, the coat that reached to his ankles, his necktie, and his derby hat were all solid black. His shirt was a crisp and starched white. He was sixty years old with a shriveled face from which his lips protruded and his bright eyes shone. The gold rings, each with a different colored stone in the settings, which he wore on every finger of both hands, were at odds with his otherwise somber appearance.

Conrad Power and Fay Reeves had both spoken of Gene Stanton's pride. It had suffered a bad blow last night and the lawman could not conceal a grimace of disgust as he raised his right hand from the belt to refasten the buttons of his jacket.

"I'm older than you, stranger," he said softly. "And slow from not needin' to outgun a man for a long time. But everybody gets what's comin' to them—sometime, someplace."

Edge nodded. "Won't give you any argument about that, feller."

79

Stanton turned on his heels to go back to the group around the buckboard. As Edge led the mare across to the hitching rail outside the saloon entrance, he recognized the sandy-haired Jethro Lovejoy and the plump and homely Maggie Woodward in the group. The dog collar and cassock worn by a tall and thin, grey-faced man named him as Flint, the town parson. There were half a dozen other men Edge did not recognize but, from their look of substance and the anxious expressions on their faces, he guessed they were members of the town council or candidates for office.

Harry Grant broke into an awkward run back towards his livery.

Meek snapped at his two helpers to continue with the chore of moving the corpses.

People began to appear on the streets in front of the small houses at the fringes of Democracy. Some on foot but many more on horseback or driving buckboards. A few headed for the midtown area, but most moved out along the trails, apparently going to their sections of the confiscated Big-B spread.

Edge hitched the mare and stepped across the sidewalk into the saloon. The many eyes directed at his back felt like a tangible pressure against his hard flesh.

The Negro had cleared away the detritus of his night's vigil and was behind the bar counter. "Man, I really thought the gent was gonna go for his gun, mister," he rasped, wiping a line of tense sweat from his top lip. "Cost him a lot not to."

"Saved him something, too," Edge answered. "His life. Who are the Kerwins?"

He reached the bar and leaned a hip against it, so that he was facing the entrance from the lobby and sideways-on to the doorway from the street.

Power swallowed hard. "Why?"

The lean, dark brown face of the half-breed showed a

80

cold smile. "Know who my friend is, feller. Like to know my enemies."

"The gent sent for the Kerwin gang?"

"McQuigg was in no position to lie."

"Jesus! Nate, Cass, and Tim Kerwin, mister! Meanest three sons any woman ever give birth to. You must've heard of them?"

"Just now. Keep talking."

"On the run from over Kansas and Missouri way. Work alone or sometimes have up to twenty men ridin' with them. Banks, railroads, stages . . . they'll hit anywhere there's big money to be took. Knew they was around this neck of the woods a while back. Heard they lit out for California, though."

"Seems they've been told there's easy pickings in Democracy," Edge answered.

"Then I reckon we're finished," Power said miserably after a long pause. "Even if Dan Warren brings in help, ain't nothin' can go up against the Kerwin gang. Short of the U.S. cavalry, maybe."

"Up to you, feller," Edge invited.

"What?"

"If you're finished, so is my job. Throw in with the majority and you won't need protecting any more."

Just for a moment, the handsome young Negro seemed to be giving the point serious consideration. But then, outside on the intersection, a man said loudly:

"Wise move, Gene! We'll do nothing until your new deputies reach town!"

Hatred gleamed in the red-rimmed eyes of the black man, and the silent snarl was made more potent as the lips curled back to display his teeth, very white in contrast with his dark skin.

"Ain't just me that needs protectin' from what that fat-bellied Snyder is doin' to this town, mister!" The words were rasped between the clenched teeth. "Every-

81

one here who ain't thrown in with him needs it. Even if most of them don't know it!"

As footfalls sounded in the lobby, Edge gave a short nod and pushed away from the bar. He was halfway to the open double doors when a group of men halted to block his path.

Frank Snyder was at the center. He looked shorter and fatter when he was standing. About forty, he had a strong-looking face with a fine bone structure. Below his hat brim was a high forehead, deep-set, dark brown eyes, a pointed nose between slightly convex cheeks, a full mouth, and a jutting jawline. The cold of the morning air had put a little color into his pale complexion.

It was almost a lean face, in comparison with his build. His shoulders were broad and his arms and legs had a puffy look. The frock coat he wore fitted him snugly, contouring breasts like those of a matronly woman and a belly that was unhealthily bulbous. He wheezed, rather than breathed.

"The name is Snyder, sir," he greeted, the lines of a scowl cut into his flesh. "Frank Snyder. Known locally as Frank and Honest Snyder. Because that is precisely what I am."

The dead-eyed Stanton and grey Reverend Flint stood on one side of Snyder. Jethro Lovejoy and a stocky, rat-faced man flanked him on the other side. The sheriff was grim, the others anxious.

"I've read the ads, feller," Edge answered.

"My campaign posters and banners, sir. In connection with tomorrow's election, which is no concern of yours. But you have chosen to make it your concern. Violently throwing in your lot with an opposition to me which is not beneath bank robbery and murder to gain its ends."

His dark eyes switched from Edge to Power and back again.

"Mr. Edge," the Reverend Flint said quickly. "And

82

you, Conrad. You should know that the entire present town council is joined with Mr. Snyder and his party in being behind the sheriff in this matter."

Lovejoy and the rat-faced man nodded their agreement.

"As I said last night," the mayor augmented, "we cannot condone violence. We would rather stand down than win by gettin' blood on our hands."

"But violence has been thrust upon us!" Snyder said pompously. "And I give you fair warning it will be combated with like."

"We already heard the gent's sent for the Kerwin gang," Power growled.

The news and the tone of voice in which it was given brought a fleeting smile to Snyder's face. Then the scowl was back. "And I can confirm that. Also, I can reveal something in addition. That, when these gentlemen arrive in town, they will be deputized. Any lawbreakers still in Democracy will be arrested. Any that have already left or who elect to leave in the interim will be hunted down and brought back. All will face trial and punishment." He stared into the impassive face of the half-breed. "You have the word of Frank and Honest Snyder on that, sir!"

"Seems to me I've had a lot of words from you, feller," Edge drawled as Snyder moved into the saloon and was trailed by the others to a table.

"A politician's failing, sir," the fat man admitted with smiling ruefulness as he sat down. "We tend to talk too much."

The others sat at the same table.

"A bottle and five glasses, Conrad!" Stanton demanded.

"It might be interesting to know your political views, sir," Snyder posed.

"They're all right," Edge supplied as the Negro

banged a bottle of whiskey and some glasses on to a tin tray.

"That's all?" Snyder asked.

"I got nothing left to say," the half-breed replied, continuing toward the lobby.

"Whiskey for the big wheels of Democracy!" Power growled, coming out from behind the bar counter, the laden tray balanced on one hand.

"You got a big mouth, black man!" Stanton snapped, then curled his lips back to show a cruel smile. "I'll remember to paint it open when I do the picture of you on the end of a rope. Guess you'll be holdin' real still for me then."

"Ignore him, Gene!" Snyder said sharply, then moderated his tone. "Let's get down to the coalition talk."

Up in his room, Edge gathered his gear together and carried it out and downstairs. He went on to the street through the hotel's main entrance.

It was gone eight now, but no warmer than it had been at dawn. The stage pulled away from in front of the depot, rolling across the intersection and heading south down Main Street towards the start of the trail to Cheyenne. The driver, shotgun, and passengers peered down at the half-breed with concealed curiosity. All the stores were open and doing steady business. But women with shopping baskets over their arms and men loading buckboards and saddlebags with supplies pointedly avoided looking at Edge as he saddled the bay mare and lashed his bedroll on behind.

Nobody spoke to him until he had led the animal down an alley between the hotel and Snyder's Dry Goods store, and into a stable there. One stall was already occupied, by a big white gelding.

"That's the gent's horse," Conrad Power said from the entrance. "Stanton's been a resident guest at the Palace for as long as I can remember. This here's Mal Tillson."

The schoolteacher stepped into view at the doorway. Like every other present or would-be town councillor Edge had so far seen, Tillson was advanced into middle age. He was beyond fifty-five, slightly built, with stooped shoulders and thinning brown hair. From the way the sallow skin hung in folds on his face and at his throat, he had obviously once been a fleshy man who had slimmed down.

"I am not a hero, Mr. Edge," he said sadly. "But neither am I a fool to be taken in by Frank Snyder's empty promises of Democracy as a land of milk and honey."

"I told him it ain't political with you, mister," Power said. "And that you don't owe him anythin'."

"School starts soon," Tillson muttered, glancing nervously around the yard between the rear of the hotel and the stable. "If there's anything I can do, I'll be there."

He scuttled away.

"One more friend," the Negro pointed out. "They're few and far between—until Dan Warren gets back to town."

"He got a gun?" Edge asked as he emerged from the stable, carrying his rifle.

A shake of the head. "The gent and his helpers collected them all up and locked them in one of the cells at the law office."

"Except that cannon of yours, uh?"

A pale imitation of Power's familiar grin showed on the dark face. "Wasn't nobody knew I had that piece under the counter, mister. Until last night. And it ain't there now." He became anxious again. "Where you goin'?"

He hurried to catch up with Edge in the alley shade between the hotel and the store.

"Have myself a shave. Figure you'll be okay until Stanton's new help arrives."

85

"No doubt about that, mister. Lovejoy and the others are only throwin' in with Snyder if things get done legal. Won't nothin' happen until after the Kerwins and their gang are deputized."

They emerged on to the street and Edge was again totally ignored by the citizens of Democracy going about their business.

"Look at the crazy bastards!" Power snarled softly, raking the intersection and the four streets leading off it with angry eyes. "Like stinkin' sheep waitin' to be fleeced soon as Snyder gets this place in his pocket! In hock up to their necks to Larry Swan! Happy for the fat man that he's livin' it up in style out at the Warren ranch house! Lookin' no further than the lousy town picnic Snyder plans to spring for soon as the election's over! Honest, decent folks for years. Until the fat man sweet-talked them with all his frank and honest bullshit!"

Edge listened impassively to the soft-spoken, bitter tirade. Then, after a heavily laden flatbed wagon had rolled past, he canted the Winchester to his left shoulder and moved out to cross the street. The hard-packed mud of the street broke up under the iron rims of the wheels, and dust rose.

"Makes you wonder if the likes of these folks are worth fightin' for, don't it?" the Negro called after him, loud enough for many passers-by to hear him.

"Who asked you, nigger?" the wagon driver snarled as he steered his team around the corner on to the north section of Main Street.

"We're nothin' to you!" a somberly clad old woman shrieked as she came out of the dry goods store. "All you care about is hangin' on to that hotel of yours!"

"Won't no one own nothin' they ain't worked for after Frank Snyder takes office!" a young man added.

Edge stepped up on to the sidewalk on the other side of the street. An elderly man in a white apron stepped out of the doorway of Young's Drugstore. "The old order's passing, son," he said sadly. "Reason we're throwing in with Snyder."

A man in the same mid-sixties age group stuck his head out of a second-story window of the newspaper office on the other side of the barber's shop. "It's the will of the people, young feller," he called down, his tone and expression as melancholy as those of the druggist.

Edge glanced back across the street, to where Conrad Power continued to glower his disgust at the town, while the grim faces of Snyder and his supporters could be seen behind a saloon window.

"Way things are shaping," he muttered, "be wise for everyone in this town to think about his will."

As he pushed open the door to the barber's shop, a bell jangled. The place was empty and no one appeared in response to the bell. He lowered himself into the center of three chairs and rested the rifle across the high arms as he leaned his head against the padding.

In the mirror, his face showed a pensive expression. The sunlight which streamed in through the window showed up every line deep cut into the dark brown flesh. The semicircular ones beneath his brooding, hooded eyes: those which ran across his forehead, dipped only slightly at the center; the others which curved away from the sides of his mouth, some to swing down to his jaw and some sweeping up over his faintly hollow cheeks.

Many were inscribed by the aging process of the passing years. But far more were the result of the bitterness and suffering experienced during those years: the scars carried by a face from which a frown, a scowl, or a snarl was seldom absent.

Perhaps there had been a brush with death or an experience of evil—his own life preserved at the expense of another—for every line visible on the reflected image of

87

his face. Or maybe the lines had been formed early and merely been deepened by the violence of passing time.

Would there be new scars if he survived whatever was in store for him in Democracy? Or would those that existed be sunk deeper into the weathered flesh?

Then again, maybe he would emerge physically unscathed. As a reward—or, at least, a token acknowledgment—for the first unselfish stand he had taken in a very long time.

For he had come to the troubled town of Democracy with a prime motive that was totally altruistic. The excuse of clearing himself with Stanton about the shootout at the way station was immaterial—and a lie. And his determination to pay back the debt he owed Conrad Power was a side issue.

He had come because he felt sympathy for Dan and Laura Warren. Knowing only the vaguest details of their trouble, he had gunned down two lawmen, basing his trust in the Warrens on their trust in him. He had been a complete stranger to them, yet Dan Warren had confessed the bank robbery and admitted there was seventy-five thousand dollars in the suitcase.

No, it had not been sympathy. Edge's capacity to feel such an emotion had been negated long ago. Rather, an affinity which was far stronger than sympathy could ever be. Powerful enough for him to commit himself to the extent of killing Hogan and Danvers before he confirmed that his trust of the Warrens was justified.

There was nothing new in the half-breed acting first and asking questions afterwards. Except to the extent that, since the opening days of the war, he had never done so unless he stood to gain: materially or otherwise. He had never done anything unless for this reason.

Yet here he sat, in the stove-heated barber shop of a town that meant nothing to him, waiting to put his life on the line. Not for money, nor revenge, nor even for a cause that was the motivating factor of many others who were involved.

He was there simply because a man had looked into the face that was reflected in the mirror and had seen something behind the surface shell of hardness and evil. Something he had considered worthwhile—worthy of trust.

The bell above the door jangled again.

And Edge smiled wryly at his reflection. So maybe he was in Democracy for his own ends. To find out something about himself he did not know.

"You got a damn nerve, mister!" the rat-faced man who had been in the saloon whined. "Comin' in here to my place. Of all the cheek . . ."

"My nerve I'll take care of myself, feller," Edge told him. "I got two cheeks and a jaw. Be obliged if you'd attend to the bristles on them."

Jay Bailey raked anxious eyes out over the street, but saw nothing or nobody there to help him. So he closed the door, took his white smock from a peg beside it, and approached the half-breed. His hands shook and his small, bright eyes darted everywhere without looking at Edge as he draped his customer's shoulders with a cloth and got some hot water from the stove.

"A man like you should support the ideals that Frank Snyder and the rest of us are workin' for," he said at length, as he stropped the razor on a leather. "Fair shares for all. You don't look like you ever got much of a share of anythin'."

"Most times I had enough, feller," Edge answered. "When I wanted more, I worked for it."

"And others always had more," Bailey countered quickly, warming to his subject as he began to lather the lean face. "Most of 'em not havin' to work for what they had."

"What other people have ain't none of my business,

89

feller. How come the stage called at the abandoned way station?"

Bailey grimaced at this reminder of sudden and violent death. "Indian trouble, mister. Bunch of drunken Sioux braves tried to stop the stage. Just a half dozen of 'em, too liquored up to shoot straight. The old stage stop was the only cover around. The white folks saw off 'em redskins pretty quick. Nicked a couple, it seems. Found the dead deputies."

He started to use the razor on Edge's bristles and the half-breed enjoyed the luxury of somebody else shaving him. Jay Bailey was good at his job.

"Hired guns with badges, the way I heard it," Edge answered after the barber had finished removing the bristles from his throat.

"Gene Stanton told us who they were, mister," Bailey replied grimly. "Men he'd come up against when he was a peace officer over in Kansas just after the war."

"Same as the new bunch?"

"Right. And you're proof we need that type, mister. And it figures that Dan Warren is out roundin' up more of the same." His tone altered from close to a snarl to one of near sadness. "It wasn't how we planned it to be. Just wanted to win the people's votes with the good sense of what we stand for. But Dan Warren made trouble."

He wiped the final trace of lather from Edge's face and the half-breed shook his head when Bailey picked up a carton of talc. He asked for his moustache to be trimmed back to a mere trace of one, along his top lip and drooping down at each side of his mouth.

"Heard Hogan and the others were here before Warren made trouble, feller."

A nod. "Yeah, they were. On account we didn't think Warren'd sit still while we was confiscatin' the Big-B spread. But Hogan and Nugent and 'em others—Gene could keep 'em in line easy. Gene's warned us he ain't so sure about the Kerwins and their bunch."

The shave was finished and Bailey removed the cloth from Edge's shoulders. The half-breed had seen the barber's price list tacked to a wall and he delved into a pants pocket and brought out fifteen cents as he stood up from the chair.

"Nice shave," he said as he handed over the money.

"I'm known to be good at my job, mister," the rat-faced Bailey responded. "And it's come to be that givin' advice is as much a part of a barber's job as shavin' and cuttin' hair. Guess I've made it plain enough—my advice to you?"

"Obliged," Edge said as the beat of many hooves were heard, far out to the north of Democracy. "But I always finish what I start out to do. Means I'll only leave town if I have to."

Bailey cocked his head to listen to the sound of the approaching horsemen. He sighed. "Too late, mister. You'll have to stay, seems like. Permanent. Six feet under out back of the church."

Edge pulled open the door and the bell jangled. "Don't figure to dig in more than my heels, feller," he replied softly as he stepped out on to the sidewalk.

As he crossed the intersection towards the angled entrance of the hotel, the riders entered Democracy, reining their horses to a canter and then a walk as they passed the town marker. There were about twenty of them, travel stained and weary looking from the long ride. As the dust of their gallop settled, Edge stepped up on to the hotel porch and turned to look along the north section of Main Street and draw his first impression of the newcomers.

All were dressed in long, warm coats against the chill of the morning air, the collars turned up and their hat brims pulled down. They wore gunbelts on top of their coats. They rode in an untidy group with no leader immediately apparent. Faces which were momentarily turned toward the sun, emerging from the shadows of hat brims, were darkly stubbled and dirt streaked.

Over the length of the street, few details were visible. But, even had he not known who they were, Edge thought he would have sensed the aura of menace emanating from the group: a certain knowledge that these men were looking for trouble and anxious to find it. A feeling based not so much on their number and physical appearance, but more on their combined attitude of quietly tense watchfulness as they surveyed their surroundings.

"It takes one to know one," the half-breed muttered softly to himself, steadying the Winchester against his shoulder with his free hand as he pumped the action.

"Whole lot more than one of them, Mr. Edge," Conrad Power growled as he stepped out of the lobby and onto the porch. He was holding the shotgun across his belly in two hands. There was fear on his black face as he halted alongside Edge and raked his dark eyes over the town streets. "And it seems the folks ain't happy to see any of them."

Main and the cross street had been emptying of townspeople as Edge left the barber shop for the hotel, the pace of the exodus from the open into cover quickening as the riders came closer. There were only the aged and infirm in sight now, awkward in their hurry to get off the streets. Horses stood docile at hitching rails and half-laden wagons remained parked outside the stores. Doors banged closed all over town.

"Guess it's been that way since this thing started?" Edge asked evenly as a lone man appeared on the street in the path of the newcomers. It was the tall, thin figure of Sheriff Stanton, wiping a brush on a rag as he walked loose-limbed from the law office.

"They're ordinary people," Power replied miserably. "Grab whatever's goin' but run for cover when the crap starts to fly."

The riders had reined their mounts to a halt ten yards short of where Stanton stood. Nobody moved for stretched seconds and in the bright sunlight the scene could have been a subdued version of one of the lawman's paintings. Then three of the newcomers dismounted and approached the sheriff.

A light breeze stirred through the town and the banners strung across the streets swayed and flapped. The breeze ended as abruptly as it had begun and the town clock on the front of the courthouse began to chime the hour of nine. Even when these intrusions of noise into cold silence had ended, the exchange of words between Gene Stanton and the Kerwin brothers could not be heard by Edge and Power.

"Somethin' you should know, Mr. Edge," the Negro said as Stanton turned and went back to his office.

"What's that, feller?"

"I ain't no hero."

The Kerwins remained where they were and their men stayed in the saddle behind them. All the men had seen as much of the town as they wanted for now and concentrated their attention on the two figures standing in front of the hotel entrance.

"So?" Edge asked.

"Don't know if it was a hint or not. But I followed your example, Mr. Edge. Got my horse saddled and ready to go."

Stanton reemerged on the street. He had gotten rid of the brush and rag and was carrying a cardboard carton and a burlap sack.

"Be badges in the box, Mr. Edge," Power supplied, licking his lips and swallowing hard. "Silas McQuigg was up most of the night makin' them. Money in the

93

sack, I guess. Lot more pay than most lawmen ever get, I reckon."

The tall, grey-haired sheriff confirmed the Negro's suspicions. He moved from the Kerwin brothers to the mounted men, delving into the box and the sack to distribute glinting five-pointed stars and stacks of bills.

"Something we both know for sure, Conrad," Edge growled as Stanton finished the chore and made a request that caused all the newcomers to raise their right hands.

"We're out-numbered, Mr. Edge."

The massed voices of the Kerwin gang, repeating the oath which Stanton recited, reached the hotel porch as a sour-toned mumbling.

The men dropped their hands and, at a signal from the tallest of the Kerwin brothers, the mounted members of the gang swung from their saddles. Stanton, his suit jacket unbuttoned and held back to display the ivory butt plates of his holstered Beaumont-Adams, turned slowly and started to walk along Main Street. His twenty newly appointed deputies trailed him, every one of them with a hand close to the jutting butt of a holstered revolver.

"Surrender peaceably, you men!" the elderly sheriff yelled. "And you'll get a legal trial! But we'll shoot you if we have to."

"You got somethin' in mind, Mr. Edge?" the Negro rasped in a frightened whisper.

"Staying alive and free is all."

"Won't do that fightin' this bunch on your own. And if you're waitin' for a miracle to happen, it sure don't look like God's on our side."

A gunshot exploded, the sound ringing out from the roof of the stage line depot on the northwest corner of the intersection.

"Bastard!" one of the Kerwin gang snarled as everyone

halted, eyes raking from the bullet hole in the hard-packed street a yard in front of the sheriff to the roofline of the depot.

Edge's eyes went to the same elevated spot. "Seems like somebody up there likes us," he muttered wryly.

"Enough!" the man on the roof yelled, from the cover of the sign proclaiming the name of the stage line. "No more killing!"

"Tillson!" the Negro rasped. "He must have held out on givin' up his rifle."

Revolvers came clear of holsters and every muzzle was tracked around to aim at the sign. Edge's face remained in its impassive set, giving no hint that the shot had been unexpected as his narrowed eyes swiveled in their sockets.

"What I said to them goes for you, schoolteacher!" Stanton snarled, after rasping an order to the Kerwins. "This is law business!"

Except for the large group of men on the north section of Main, the streets of Democracy continued to be empty. And, again, the half-breed concealed his feelings behind the unflinching flesh of his freshly shaved face.

"I want assurances that . . ." Tillson began.

"Go take the nigger and the drifter!" Stanton roared. "The schoolteacher won't . . ."

The tallest Kerwin held up a hand with the four fingers extended, thumb folded across the palm, and pushed it forward. He and his brothers started to walk and four of their men moved in their wake.

The barrel of a rifle appeared at the side of the sign atop the stage depot and a shot curtailed the sheriff's boast. Then another and another. More hard-packed dirt was exploded into dust as bullet holes pocked the street, this time ahead of the advancing deputies.

"Frig this!" the brother who was the obvious leader of

95

the gang snarled, whirling, dropping into a crouch and blasting a shot toward the sign.

The rest of the men were only a moment late in imitating his actions: the fusillade of shots exploded a shower of wood splinters from the sign behind which Tillson was crouched. The noise masked whatever the enraged Stanton was bellowing as he pointed toward the abruptly deserted porch of the hotel.

Beyond the open doorway, Edge was shoving an only slightly reluctant Conrad Power across the lobby and into the saloon.

"But it ain't right," the Negro complained, moving of his own free will now as he led the way behind the bar and through the archway into the rear. "Tillson ain't got a chance."

"Gave us one, though," the half-breed answered through clenched teeth as they emerged out into the yard and ran across it to the stable. "Maybe you prayed just enough, feller."

The Kerwin gang had been fanning their revolvers, pouring lead up at the roof of the stage depot. Abruptly, the firing ended.

"All right!" Tillson cried shrilly. "All right! I surrender!"

"Go get the nigger and Edge!" Stanton countered.

Running feet hit the street as the new deputies raced on to the intersection and across it.

The half-breed and Power were already astride their horses and in the yard. The deputies began to shout in a mixture of anger and glee and these additional sounds of their advance masked the beat of hooves as the two fugitives galloped their horses across the back lots of the buildings on the west side of Main Street.

Edge was in the lead now, and Power trailed him, sticking close as the half-breed veered his mount to the west. Gunshots sounded behind them. But they were the low-powered cracks of revolvers and the bullets ploughed harmlessly into the dirt, far short of the moving targets.

Then the shooting ended. Both men eased their horses from the flat-out gallop and glanced back over their shoulders. The Kerwin gang grouped out back of the Palace Hotel stable no longer looked dangerous over such a distance through settling dust. On foot and armed only with short-range weapons, they looked despondent and defeated. Beyond them, standing out starkly against the skyline on the roof of the stage depot, the slightly built, stoop-shouldered figure of Tillson eased erect, his arms held high above his head.

"A very damn small miracle," Power said breathlessly. "For all the prayin' I did."

Another man appeared on the distant rooftop, thrusting forward a handgun toward the schoolteacher. As he approached his prisoner, Gene Stanton was content not to add any more gunsmoke to that which was already drifting across Democracy.

"Maybe it was just a sign, feller," the half-breed answered evenly.

"What of?" the hotel man growled, and spat forcefully at the ground. "That when we're given the chance, we can be as yellow as everyone else in Democracy?"

There was no pursuit and the two slowed their horses still more, to an easy canter.

"You ain't yellow, feller," the half-breed said at length.

"Not on the outside, mister. I'm a nigger, like Stanton is always tellin' me. Which is maybe why Snyder and his bunch are bound to take over Democracy. 'Cause I'm on the other side and God ain't never shown no sign he likes the Negroes he created."

"Unless that was it, in your case, Conrad."

The Negro spat again. "They say He works in mysterious ways His wonders to perform, mister. But this way beats me—letting that crazy schoolteacher get caught by the gent while I take it on the run like a bat outta hell."

"You're alive and free, feller."

A shake of the handsome head. "That was what you wanted for yourself, mister. And I already told you I ain't owed it by you. So you can ride on to wherever you were headed when you come by, mister. I aim to go back to town."

"Me, too, feller. But later."

The Negro shrugged. "Sure, later. But soon, mister. You beat me, though. What's in it for you?"

"Just me." The half-breed grinned. "And nothing to do with proving I'm not yellow."

"Never thought you was."

"And neither are you, Conrad."

Now Power grinned. "Maybe if they think we are, though, it gives us the edge." He laughed out loud. "You get it?"

"Sure, feller," Edge replied. Then, as the Negro looked back again at the town in the distance: "Later, like you said. Democracy ain't ready for it, yet."

"It?" He was puzzled.

Edge grinned briefly again. "Black Power."

Chapter Eight

Edge and Conrad Power rode far to the west and then when the intervening terrain hid them from the town, they swung northward. It was after midday when the half-breed altered course again, to head east. The whole time, they were on what had once been the Warrens' Big-B spread. The families who had gone into hock to the town bank to buy pieces of the range were toiling hard in the chill sunlight.

Those whose newly purchased sections of land were close to Democracy would have seen the Kerwin gang riding into town and many would have heard the explosion of gunfire that had disturbed the morning. But the reactions of these people to the two horsemen were the same as those of the men and women working too far out in open country to be aware of what had happened. A pointed indifference. They continued to erect fences and build shacks, to plough the pastureland for planting, and to dig irrigation ditches: to look anywhere but at the black man and the half-breed riding by.

"Snyder's got them in the palm of his friggin' sticky hand!" Power snarled to end a long silence. "And ain't no use tryin' to tell the lunkheads that the fat man'll clench his fist and start squeezin' soon as their sweat starts to earn money!"

"It was tried?" Edge asked. "Telling them? I never did see any posters that weren't for Snyder's men."

Power had done a great deal of spitting along the way. But he still had plenty of saliva left. Another globule of moisture marked their route. "There was posters, mister. All over. But they got torn down soon as they went up. Them first deputies the gent brought in did the tearin' down. Didn't make no difference, though. They'd've busted up any meetin's Lovejoy and crowd got goin', I guess. But never was one. Nobody ever showed up. On account of Snyder had already sold his bill of goods to the townspeople."

Another long silence was broken by Edge. "Stanton was always with the Snyder camp, feller?"

The Negro looked about to spit again, but held back the wet and sighed with a shake of his head. "The gent was never with no one, mister. Came into town trackin' the last of a bunch of bank robbers. Trailed them all the way from Indian Territory, pickin' them off one by one. Got his last man in a showdown on Main Street. Went away with him, then came back. We didn't have no sheriff and old man Warren reckoned it would be a good idea if we did have. In the event any more outlaws tried to hole up in Democracy. So the gent was appointed to the office.

"Kept himself to himself and didn't do much else 'cept paint pictures. Until old man Warren cashed in and Frank Snyder started to stir the crap. Then his mean streak come out and he brought in the hired guns to back him."

Another shake of the head, this time with a grimace on the black face. "Ain't no doubt he was a good lawman once. But the idea of easy money from other people's sweat got to him. Same reason Snyder ain't just a fat storekeeper no more. Nor McQuigg just a fine

100

blacksmith. Nor none of the rest what they used to be. What we doin' here?"

They had been riding east on the trail from Laramie for several miles, then reached the fork and could see the derelict way station ahead of them. In the bright sunlight of afternoon the broken-down building looked even more forlorn than it had during the rainstorm of last night. The half-breed felt no sense of being watched as he rode closer, his hooded eyes spotting the bullet holes and other signs of the early morning Sioux attack.

"The Warrens went to buy help," he replied. "Last time they were seen was here."

"They sure did make it a long way on foot," Power said, with mixed sadness and admiration as he followed Edge's example and slid from the saddle. "But it'll be a cold trail to follow, mister."

They led their horses across the front of the way station and around the side to the corral at the rear. The frost and sun-hardened mud still carried the impressions from which the bodies of Hogan, Danvers, and Robarts had been lifted.

The Negro spat into each shallow indentation as he followed Edge across the corral.

The rain and wind had continued for a long time after the half-breed had ridden away from the place. The corpses had sheltered the sign they had made, but all other traces of what had happened at the way station had been obliterated by the storm. Looking in the direction he had seen the Warrens ride, Edge could see no clue that they had passed over the once muddy and now solid ground.

"They just took the money and took off?" he said softly, taking the makings from a shirt pocket and starting to roll a cigarette.

"I saw them go north," Power replied miserably. "I didn't ask no questions before we hit the bank. And weren't no time afterwards. Alarm was raised too soon. Wasn't even a chance for them to get to their horses. They just went off into the storm. But they said they'd be back. And I believe it, Mr. Edge."

He broke out some jerked beef from one of his saddle-bags and handed several pieces to the half-breed. Edge finished smoking his cigarette before he started to eat. Then both men chewed on the dried meat for a long time, not talking and becoming increasingly aware of the cold now that they were no longer on the move.

"Didn't they trust you, feller?"

The question startled the Negro and he swallowed a mouthful of softened meat before he replied. "What kinda question's that, mister? I was the only one around Democracy they did trust."

Edge nodded. "You get much trouble with the Sioux in Carroll County?"

Power found the abrupt change of subject equally surprising. But then a dull light of partial understanding showed in his dark eyes. "Not for a long time. Sometimes we heard about renegade bands raidin' over to the east. And north in the Dakotas. But that stuff with the stage this mornin'—first time somethin' like that's happened since I don' remember when."

"More than just a half-dozen braves around this part of the state, though?"

The black man had seen the half-breed's drift completely now: and the frown he expressed showed that he did not like it. He spoke softly. "Over at Whitehead Crossin' is a big meetin' place for them, mister." He raised a hand to point northeast from the broken-down corral fence. "Ten miles or so along the old trail. Always some there. Every now and then a whole bunch gather for the council." He looked hard at the impassive profile of the slowly chewing half-breed. "But just because a

102

handful of liquored-up braves took it into their head to ..."

"Just an idea, Conrad," Edge cut in quietly. "On account that Warren told me his wife used to teach at an Indian school."

Power had not eaten all the beef. He looked at what was left and suddenly lost his appetite. There was an angry set to his black face as he stuffed the dried meat into his saddlebag. And the new emotion was again displayed as he fastened the straps. When he swung up into the saddle of his black gelding and looked down at Edge, there was just a trace of how he felt visible in the set of his features.

"A good idea, mister. On your part. Should have figured it out for myself, I guess. Dan Warren don't have the same connections as Stanton. And he ain't stupid. Not stupid enough, anyway—to ride into some cattletown and advertise that he's got seventy-five grand to hire fast guns." He pursed his lips and whistled through them. "But Indians! One lousy idea. No wonder he didn't tell me. Kept stallin' me whenever I asked him what he figured to do."

Edge mounted his bay mare. "So he didn't trust you that much, uh?"

He heeled the horse forward, veering to go between a gap in the leaning fence. Power held back, debating whether or not to follow. He made his decision and urged his mount from the standstill. It took him only a few moments to catch up with the slow-riding half-breed.

"And for good reason, mister! My Pa and Ma were both killed by a bunch of liquored-up braves. When they was out on a huntin' trip in the Black Hills. First vacation they took after sweatin' out their guts buildin' the Palace."

103

"That the only one, feller?" Edge asked as they turned on to the trail, heading northeast.

"What, mister?"

"Reason."

"No, it ain't. Which is why I'm still ridin' along with you. But understand this—I ain't no Indian hater just because they're redskins." He vented a hollow laugh. "How could a nigger be that?"

"Speak your piece, Conrad," Edge invited coldly. "And I'll listen." He negated some of the harshness in his tone by curling back his lips. "Providing it ain't too colorful."

"Indians can't be trusted! It's a known fact and I've always figured they can't help bein' that way. Especially they can't be trusted when they're liquored up. And you give an Indian money, he spends it on liquor first chance he gets. Ain't that your experience, mister?"

"Ain't me who's speaking my piece right now, Conrad."

Power spat. "Hell, you know what I'm gettin' at. The big wheels back at Democracy done a bad thing bringin' in the Kerwin gang. But no one'll get hurt if they don't cause no trouble. Indians, though! If enough of them get turned loose on a white man's town, no tellin' what'll happen. A massacre. When they got war in their bellies, they don't care who they slaughter. Women and children—babies even. And even if the folks in town don't like the Kerwin gang any more than we do, they'll fight alongside them to defend Democracy."

He paused, waiting for a response from Edge. When none came, he sighed. "I tell you this, mister. I'd rather see those folks back there squeezed dry by Snyder and his crowd than murdered by liquored-up Sioux. I reckon any man deservin' of the name would."

"Dan Warren ain't a man?"

Anger was full born again in the dark eyes of the Ne-

104

gro. And each word he spoke was like a piece of flint he was spitting out. "Dan Warren ain't been thinkin' straight since he got cheated out of his spread, mister. And Laura, she's always figured that the sun shone out of every Indian's asshole. Both of them need straightenin' out—and I just hope we're in time to do that."

He heeled his gelding into a gallop, but slowed him again and looked angrily back toward Edge as the half-breed continued to hold his mare to an easy walk.

"What the hell?" he snarled. "We're already more than a day behind them!"

"Ten miles you said, feller," Edge pointed out as he drew level with Power. "It's just an idea that they went to Whitehead Crossing. If they did, they been there a long time. Waiting for the council to meet. I'm with you, Conrad. Don't trust Indians. So I don't figure to just ride up in full daylight and ask for a cup of coffee."

Because he had been carrying a heavy load of anger, it took the black man several moments to lose it. And then he showed a sheepish grin. "Dan Warren ain't the only man who don't think straight all the time, right?"

Edge dug out the makings of another cigarette and rolled and lit it before he responded. "Lots like it, Conrad. But some of them live to an old age. They either stay lucky or learn by their mistakes."

There was another long silence then, Edge smoking the cigarette and maintaining a careful surveillance of the surrounding terrain; Conrad Power staring directly ahead but wearing an expression which suggested his mind was elsewhere.

The country through which they traveled, as the sun sank behind and to the left of them, was a barren wasteland of rock, hard-packed dirt, and scrub grass. It rose and fell with gentle grades and was scattered with occa-

105

sional stands of mixed timber and rearing bluffs which were never so high as they looked from a distance.

The trail they rode along was well marked, but long disused. Here and there were the derelict remains of former farmsteads which had been abandoned by optimists who had thought the land could be made productive.

"Some of the folks who used to own these places live in Democracy now," Power said sadly. "Worked the herds for old man Warren or rented farmsteads from him. Easy to see how Snyder and his crowd were able to sweet-talk them."

"Seems to me a backward five-year-old could sell those people any damn thing, feller," Edge replied, and there was a savage tone in his voice although his expression as he continued to scan the land on all sides remained unrevealing.

"Your turn to say your piece, Mr. Edge?" Power asked, still sad. "And maybe tell me why you and me set ourselves up like ducks in a shootin' gallery when the Kerwin gang hit town?"

"To give the people one final chance to mean something in my book, Conrad!" the half-breed told him, rasping the words through clenched teeth.

"The schoolteacher said he was with us, and he was the only one ready to do anythin' when the crap started to fly." A shrug. "He surprised me, Mr. Edge. But I wasn't surprised at all when no one else backed us up. I could've told you. You didn't have to set yourself up to be blasted."

"Do things my way, Conrad."

" 'Cause you don't trust nobody?"

"Maybe because I want to live to be an old man. Or know the reason why I'm dying when I die."

Power nodded, looking wise and sad. "And if you cash in around here, it'll be on account of a bunch of folks

106

whose backbones got melted by greed. Folks who want everythin' and don't care how they get it—long as they don't get hurt."

There was another lengthy silence. The sun turned red as it began to slide behind the distant mountains in the west, and a breeze sprang up, attacking exposed flesh with a sample of the night's intense cold to come.

Edge called a halt in the lee of a low bluff and set a small fire. They stewed some of the jerked beef and ate it with hot coffee to wash it down. The stop was only long enough to prepare and eat the meal. Then they set off again, Edge taking the lead and swinging a half mile to the south before turning to ride parallel with the trail.

An hour later, with the moon and stars bright and glinting against a matt black sky, a dome of orange showed above a bluff ahead and to the left.

"That'll be Whitehead Crossin'," the Negro said tensely. "Big fire's gotta mean a big bunch of Sioux, I guess."

Edge did not reply until they had ridden another five hundred yards to a stand of timber, the trees canting to the south as a result of a stronger wind than the one blowing tonight. He dismounted and tethered the mare to a branch.

"With sentries posted, feller," he said, watching Power slide from the saddle. "If it's war talk."

He slid the Winchester from the boot and the black man unhooked the strap of the shotgun from around his saddlehorn.

"A war that never had anythin' to do with you, Mr. Edge. Dan Warren wants it. The Snyder bunch asked for it. The ordinary folks back in Democracy don't deserve to be saved from it. 'Ceptin' by a man who cares enough about them." He spat into the tough grass at which the horses were cropping. "Which I do. But you don't give a shit for them, mister."

107

"Right, Conrad," Edge agreed.

"So why are you here? Could be I don't trust you, mister!" It was a loud snarl.

There was menace in Power's voice and when Edge glanced at him he saw the suspicion carved into the handsome young face of the Negro. But the shotgun was held loosely in two hands across Power's belly, hammers at the rest and pointing at no target.

The half-breed's Winchester was held in the same manner, but the expression on the lean face was nonchalant as he started to turn. It was a slow, casual movement—which suddenly exploded into high-speed violence.

Thinking Edge was about to lead the way on foot through the timber, Power leaned forward, thrusting out a foot.

He had time to vent a roar of anger and alarm, but not to draw back or bring up the shotgun.

For Edge had powered into a forceful whirl, tilting the rifle to bring the stock to shoulder height. His hands tightened into hard fists around the frame and barrel and the full impetus of his turn was behind the crack of wood against the black man's jaw.

The blow curtailed Power's roar, but Edge did not accept this. As the Negro staggered to the side and corkscrewed to the ground, he followed him down, bending from the waist and prepared to use the rifle stock again.

But the Negro was out cold, the shotgun slipping from his opening hands. The broad chest of the man was unmoving for a stretched second. Then began to rise and fall, the breath rattling in his throat.

The half-breed rested his rifle against a tree trunk and worked with smooth speed. He used the lariat from Power's saddle and his razor to cut lengths of rope and tie the black man—first the ankles, then the wrists behind the back, then the ankles to the wrists. Not tight

108

enough for the rope to cut into the flesh or for the shoulders and legs of the Negro to be drawn taut.

The man's breathing was less labored when Edge straightened up from him, returning the razor to the neck pouch and retrieving the Winchester.

"No sweat, Conrad," he said, lips curling back and eyes narrowing to form what was almost a warm smile. "Now I trussed you."

Chapter Nine

AS Edge made fast but careful progress towards the bluff with the fireglow beyond it, he was no longer smiling. But he felt no sense of regret for what he had done to Conrad Power. He knew the Negro would wake to pain, then anger: perhaps even a little regret of his own. But then he would see the two horses still tethered to the tree branch—probably before he had time to experience fear. Then the anger would return, mixed in with a great deal of resentful wondering.

It was not the Negro's motives which the half-breed distrusted. Instead, the black man's ability to achieve what he had set out to do. For Power was a hotel man with a belief and guts: determination and a shotgun. All of these things useless—and even disadvantageous—if it was not tempered with experience.

So Edge had elected to work alone, closing in on the Sioux encampment, treading silently and constantly alert to react to the first sight or sound that would indicate sentries were posted. He had made such an approach toward an Indian stronghold before—more than once—either alone or in the company of men who shared his skills and abilities. And who, above all else, considered their own skins of prime importance.

Birdcalls, slightly off-key, were the first signs of posted sentries. They were passed along in a four-part relay at the base of the bluff. Edge was stationary on the blind side of a low rise when he heard the signals. He backtracked down the hill and veered to the south in a crouch, zigzagging to take advantage of every chance at cover. All around him, trees, brush, and grass swayed under the tug of the icy breeze. And, like an Indian himself, he used the motion of weather against natural formations to conceal his own movements.

His progress was slow and arduous and, all the time, fear stayed a cold ball in the pit of his stomach. Beads of sweat were like pinpricks of ice under his armpits, at the base of his spine, and in the creases of his throat.

From the southern end of the bluff he was able to see the crouched forms of two Sioux braves. Moonlight glinted dully on the barrels of their rifles. Four more birdcalls sounded as the sentries reported to each other that they were still unharmed and on watch.

Edge left them unaware of his passing and worked his way around the bluff, to the slope on the far side. He had no way of knowing whether the council had posted a second line of sentries and continued his advance on the assumption they they had. Slow and careful, as before. Surviving from instinct and practice. Caring only about his own life, because if he lost that, everything was lost.

Conrad Power would not have been in such a compassionless frame of mind had he not been forced to remain back in the stand of timber. Even had he got this far, by curbing his impatience and learning in a few moments how to outwit Indians by adopting their own tactics, his mind would have been concerned with others and how he could achieve the high ideal of saving them.

He could not have crouched behind a rock, seen the evil that was being done to Fay Reeves, and remained as impassively detached from the harrowing scene as was Edge.

111

The half-breed had moved across the slope, inching forward on his belly to gain the vantage point in cover of a scattering of boulders. Spread out below him was the Sioux meeting place, sited at a point where the old stage trail forded a narrow, shallow stream. Once, there had been a way station at the ford, but it had long ago fallen or been torn down so that now only the outline of the building foundations remained.

There was a rope corral containing some fifty ponies on the other side of the stream. Beyond this, about three hundred yards from where Edge crouched, were a score of tepees, erected in a wide circle around the blazing fire.

To one side of the fire, which leapt with flames and billowed with smoke at the dictates of the strengthening wind, a large group of braves daubed with warpaint and wearing bonnets were seated before the tallest tepee. Close by two wagons were parked, each with a team of four horses in the traces. They were flatbeds, pressed low on their springs, their freight securely covered by canvas sheeting lashed tightly in place.

There were no raised voices at the council and the crackling of the fire was the only sound from the camp which reached the ears of the watching Edge.

The whore from Democracy was too exhausted to utter more than a mild protest at each degrading humiliation which was forced upon her by the Indians—braves and squaws—not engaged in the council. She was naked and spread-eagled on the ground, wrists and ankles tied to short stakes. Without the restrictions of her heavily boned undergarments, her torso was full-blown, the belly bulbous and breasts sagging under their no longer conical weight. But her upper arms looked almost slim in comparison with her flabby thighs.

Her nudity and suffering were plain to see in the

112

bright firelight. But the half-breed was too far away, and at a crosswind to her, so he could not smell her.

She had been raped many times, that was obvious, from the semen-diluted blood crusted on her lower belly and thighs. And her bruised and torn lips showed that not only her womb had been sexually violated. But such assaults had ceased long ago. Whatever sexual attraction the naked Fay Reeves had held for the Sioux braves had been obliterated by their own lust. Now, whenever a brave or a squaw approached the helpless whore, it was to stand or crouch over her—to empty bladder or bowels over flesh already run with wet and filth.

Whether she opened her mouth and expelled silence or a croaking plea, Edge was unable to tell. He looked at her specifically only briefly, then surveyed the entire camp with the whore registered in his mind as a single detail.

Then he left the security of the rocks to move closer, the scene and what was missing from it firmly set in his mind. The absent factors were Dan and Laura Warren.

Sentries were posted on every side of the campsite, but there was just the one circle of them. Edge was through the defensive ring and the Sioux below him—whether in council or listlessly awaiting the result of the talk—had faith in their guards.

The birdcall signals continued. The warriors talked. Fay Reeves suffered in silence under the stink of others' waste. The squaws and the braves not invited to the council either lost interest in the whore or were unable to torment her further in such a disgusting manner.

Edge worked his way across and down the slope and reached the foundations of the old way station. The stream made gentle bubbling noises as it flowed over its rock bed. The fire crackled. Talk was exchanged by the group in front of the tallest tepee. But even had the language been English or Spanish, he doubted if he would

113

have been able to comprehend more than the occasional word.

The smell of Fay Reeves was strong enough to reach between the tepees and cross the stream to assault the half-breed's nose. More potent and far more sickening than that emanating from the horse droppings in the nearby rope corral.

"You are good, White Eyes," a voice said softly behind the prone half-breed. "But born the wrong color in the wrong place."

He turned just his head, screwing his neck far around to peer over his shoulder. The brave was young. No more than eighteen. The only paint he wore on his face was dark, to merge with the night. Like the other Sioux Edge had already seen, he was dressed in somber-hued buckskin leggings, shirt, and mocassins. A blanket was wrapped around his torso and out of this he pointed a Winchester rifle. He was squatting on his haunches and looked as if he had been positioned thus for some time. His English was good.

"All the way in, uh?" Edge asked, letting go of his own rifle so that the gun rested on the rotted remains of the way station floor.

"I watched you for a long time. Made sure you were alone. You did not come here to die."

"There must be better places and better ways, feller," the half-breed answered.

A nod. "One man could kill one man. Perhaps two or three. What I think. So you just scout."

He rose to his full height and gestured for Edge to do likewise. The half-breed complied.

"Pretty lousy one, it seems."

A shake of the head this time. "I am not sentry posted by Blue Moon. Not considered worthy. You fooled those considered worthy. Now the chief will have to consider me."

114

There was another gesture with the rifle and Edge turned away from the young brave and started to ford the stream. The icy water was never more than knee deep.

The approach of the prisoner and escort was seen and a shout went up. Then many voices were raised. The council came to an abrupt end amid excited noise and fast movement. Then, as Edge was shepherded between two tepees and into the firelit circular area, a single voice boomed out above all the others. The silence it commanded came instantly, but the activity continued until all the Indians were in a position to see Edge—in a semicircle at the side of the fire where Fay Reeves was staked out.

"Stop, White Eyes!" the young brave ordered and Edge complied, a few feet from the whore's head.

"They've sent me crazy," she croaked, her punished-lips hardly moving as she swiveled her eyes high in their sockets to gain an upside-down view of the half-breed. "It ain't really you, feller."

"It's me, ma'am," Edge told her without looking at her. "Which maybe means I'm the one that's crazy."

He was ignoring her to look at the Indian who wore the most ornate bonnet and vivid warpaint. He was in his midthirties, with a handsome face and strong look-ing, solid build. The braves had parted to allow him through and he halted with his back to the fire, apprais-ing the intruder with dark eyes that gave nothing away.

"He came alone, Chief Blue Moon," the brave with the Winchester reported, voice filled with pride. "With great skill he came through the sentries and watched the camp from the remains of the ancient building. I, John Elk, captured him."

A brave in the tightly packed group of watchers was speaking in his native tongue, translating the English for those who did not understand the language.

Blue Moon folded his arms and acknowledged the report with a curt nod. He did not take his impassive gaze off Edge. "Why?" He had a deep voice which even speaking this single word, not loudly, had a booming quality. Then, before the half-breed could answer, he unfolded his arms and pointed to the naked and evil-smelling Fay Reeves. "For her?"

The whore had spirit. Despite everything that had happened to her, she had what it took to inject sarcasm into her tone. "Fat chance."

"Guess she did something real bad to you people?" Edge asked evenly.

His hooded eyes had taken only a moment to survey Blue Moon. Then he had glanced around the camp at close quarters with apparent nonchalance. The braves and squaws were as undemonstrative of their feelings as the chief. Beyond those on Edge's left, standing at the entrance of a tepee, two faces were very expressive. The white faces of Dan and Laura Warren: whiter, anyway, than those of the Sioux Indians. Although the woman's was smudged with dirt and her husband's was dirtier still and heavily stubbled.

"She was attacked by one of my braves," Blue Moon replied. "He was drunk. Firewater and lust lost him his manhood."

"I cut off his balls, feller," Fay Reeves croaked. "With his own knife while he was sleepin' off what he done to me."

Edge was no longer looking at the Warrens. He had seen that the good-looking redhead was anxious to intervene and that her fleshy husband had held her back, with a scowl, a snarled word, and a tight grip on her upper arm.

"Been done to you before," the half-breed muttered, the main symptom of his fear still a hard, cold ball in

116

the pit of his stomach. But the heat of the fire kept his sweat warm.

"Not out in the open in the middle of the lousy night," the whore retorted in a low-voiced snarl. "And never for free."

"For this she suffers so," Blue Moon boomed softly. "As a white man's woman of pleasure her crime was greater than that of the brave who attacked her. But she has been punished enough."

The hand pointed again. But it shot out with greater speed, snatching at the weapon belt and, at the full extent of the arm's reach, releasing a knife.

"I should've . . ." the whore started.

Then the blade ceased to spin, the force of the underarm throw burying four inches of the glinting metal into the flabby flesh of Fay Reeves. Its target was just beneath the heavy left breast. The death rattle sounded in her throat, she spasmed once and became still. Her punished mouth gaped wide and her eyes remained open, still swiveled high to stare at Edge.

"Oh, dear God!" Laura Warren shrieked, but was still captive in the firm grip of her husband.

Blue Moon curled back his lips in a cruel smile as he refolded his arms. "She suffers no more, White Eyes. Is there reason why you should not suffer?"

"You'll have to give me time to think of one, feller," Edge answered flatly.

"Blue Moon!" Dan Warren shouted, the words sounding as if they had to squeeze past something hard in his throat. "Edge helped us get the money to you!"

The satanic smile was wiped from the chief's painted face and replaced by confusion. It lasted for perhaps two seconds. Then he shrugged.

"Laura has never lied to the Indian," he told Edge. "And we believe her when she says we can trust man who wedded her. So be it. But you must surrender your revolver . . . Edge?"

"You've got the name right," the half-breed confirmed, then unbuttoned his coat and held it back, offering access to the holstered Colt.

"Thank God," Laura Warren gasped.

John Elk had picked up Edge's Winchester and held it and his own rifle under an arm as he moved up behind the half-breed and claimed the handgun.

When the young brave had backed away, Blue Moon issued a string of orders in his native tongue. The group broke up. The council reassembled in front of the chief's tepee. A half-dozen braves went to the rear of one of the wagons. A rope was unfastened, the cover was lifted, and each drew a Winchester and carton of shells from beneath it. John Elk pushed Edge's Winchester and Colt under the canvas, then joined the council. The other braves left the camp to reinforce the sentries. The squaws and remaining braves moved into tepees. Edge could sense their watchful eyes on him as Dan Warren walked slowly out of the shadow of the tepee and into the ring of fireglow.

"It happened on the trail from Democracy," the dispossessed owner of the Big-B spread said morosely. "Just the way the chief said it did. There was a little time to talk after the brave she castrated brought her into camp."

"The way we've got time to talk, feller?" Edge asked.

Warren looked sick with exhaustion. The shrug he gave seemed to take a lot of effort. "Talk's all we can do, Edge. Laura and me are as much prisoners as you are. Out of our hands, what they decide."

He nodded miserably towards the council. Then looked back at the naked corpse of Fay Reeves. Blue Moon's knife was still buried in her heart, the slight ooze of blood around the blade already congealed. But the

118

eyes watching from out of the shadowed interiors of the tepees were a potent warning against trying to withdraw the weapon.

"She heard Stanton was bringing in the Kerwin gang. Seems she was Nathan Kerwin's woman in Kansas City a few years back. Ran out on him one day and took his bankroll with her—along with the latest bruises he'd given her. Scared the hell out of her when she heard the Kerwins were headin' for town." He sighed, wrinkling his nose at the stench rising from the corpse. "Maybe she'd have been better off stayin' in Democracy and takin' whatever he planned to give her."

"Dan!" Laura called.

"No way we could've stopped them, Edge," Warren muttered. "Would have, if there'd been a chance. Whore or not, I always felt sorry for Fay. In all her life, nothin' ever went right for her, I guess."

The half-breed shot a final glance down at the filth-streaked corpse before moving to follow Warren. "She sure got fouled up in the end, feller," he drawled.

Chapter Ten

LIGHT and warmth from the fire penetrated into the tepee. So did the words being spoken at the council assembly. Laura Warren listened to what was being said outside, apparently able to shut from her mind the voice of her husband. Horror at the brutal death of Fay Reeves was gone from her weary face. She now expressed deep misery as she hugged herself and stared at Edge who, like the Warrens, was seated on a folded blanket.

"There was nothin' else we could do," her husband explained in a tone of pleading. "Stanton brought in the gunmen and threatened to send for more. Nobody in Democracy cared. Nobody would fight. Laura came up with the idea of askin' the Sioux for help. But I ain't blamin' her, Edge." His tone suddenly quickened. "I went right along with the idea. We were desperate."

The half-breed continued to listen without revealing a reaction to what he was hearing. They had asked him no questions and he had remained silent since entering the tepee. First he had surveyed the interior and seen it contained nothing except the blankets and two tin plates on which the leftovers of a meal had hardened. The Warrens were dressed in the same manner as they had been at the abandoned way station. But Dan no longer had the Winchester.

"But it's been a long time since Laura taught school on the reservations. Times have changed and so've the young bucks Laura used to learn."

He gazed out at the flames and smoke, whirling and leaping in the wind.

"Blue Moon was here when we came," he continued at length. "And a handful of others. Laura knows him from when she give lessons to his kids. He said he'd help. Took the money and sent the braves off, every which way. When this many showed up—with two wagonloads of guns and ammo and liquor—we knew he'd made suckers outta us."

"But we'll be all right," his wife put in, her expression and the direction of her gaze not altering. "The talk's almost over. They'll start drinking soon. Some of them want to kill us, but Blue Moon doesn't want that. Some others, too. Those who came to my schools. I think there's enough of them so that we'll be safe."

Suddenly, she blinked and looked harder at Edge—almost as if she had been staring sightlessly at him before and only now saw him. "Why did you come here, Mr. Edge? How did you know where to come?"

There were loud voices outside and fast moving shadows against the flickering firelight. Braves used knives to cut free the bonds at the whore's wrists and ankles. She was dragged away. Other braves hacked at the ropes of both wagons. Bottles clinked against each other. Harsh laughter punctuated the excited talk.

"Came because I figured there was nowhere else you could go. Unless you were planning to just go and not come back. Conrad Power pointed me in the right direction."

"Conrad knew?" Warren gasped.

"Not until I told him."

"What did he . . . ? Where is he . . . ?"

Edge showed a brief, cold smile. "He's tied up right now."

"Why?" Laura insisted. "Why did you come? The money?"

"There was an easier time and place for that, ma'am. No, came to see if I could stop this happening." He waved a hand toward the scene outside the tepee. Then pursed his lips. "But nobody wins them all."

"For what, Mr. Edge. Why should you care?"

Edge looked away from her steady gaze, out of the entrance to an area beside the fire where six tepee poles were being driven into the ground. "Thought I did care, Mrs. Warren," he replied softly. "My mistake. Came here to try to correct it."

The stocky figure of Chief Blue Moon blocked the entrance. He did not have to stoop far to peer inside. "Laura?"

"Yes?"

"You heard what was said and told them, Laura?"

"That you will not harm us, Blue Moon."

The chief nodded. "That is good. But I fear you will suffer, even though I and many others of my tribe would not wish it. For many White Eyes will die as a result of your actions, Laura. The money which you have given us has bought guns. It will buy more guns. From White Eyes who think nothing of how the guns will be used. But you are not like this, Laura. And I do not think you would wed a man like this. So you will suffer. And your husband. Perhaps your friend. Your own minds will make you suffer. For this, I am sorry."

"Then stop it, for God's sake!" Warren pleaded.

Laura laid a hand on his arm. "Dan, he could not do that. Even if he wanted to."

Blue Moon nodded. "It is as Laura says. I have given my people my word. For too long we have awaited such an opportunity. Tomorrow, we will destroy your town

122

and all who are in it. We will be joined after our victory by other brothers from all over this land. And then we will kill or drive out every White Eyes on this land. And it will be ours again."

Warren had craned his head to the side to see around the chief. "What's happenin'?" he demanded.

As Blue Moon stepped aside, Laura Warren answered for him. "A decision of the council, Dan. Those braves stole guns and alcohol from the supplies. Then tried to hold up the stage from Laramie. They are to be punished for acting without permission."

The six braves had been led from a tepee, their hands tied behind their backs. Then lashed, at ankles and necks, to the poles driven into the ground. As the chief moved so that the occupants of the tepee had an uninterrupted view of the scene, the shirts of the tied men were ripped and cut from their bodies.

The brave who had raped Fay Reeves could be singled out from the large, dark stain at the crotch of his leggings. He was close to unconsciousness, his head rolling from side to side, his chin on his chest. The others held themselves rigidly erect, obviously terrified but attempting, in the Indian manner, to face their punishment with a stubborn pride in their ability to endure pain. All of them were young, between the ages of sixteen and twenty.

"Even when you taught them, Laura," Blue Moon said sadly, "you always knew what the Sioux had done in the past. And what they were capable of doing again in the future."

The woman nodded, tight-lipped.

"She was betting seventy-five grand on it," Edge muttered.

Most of the Indians were in a semicircle to one side of the fire again. But they were seated on the hard-packed dirt and were not silent. Many voices contributed to a

123

low, excited buzz. Bottles were raised to lips and lowered. Pipes of tobacco were passed along the line.

"I heard Stanton was paying his hired guns twenty dollars a day, Mr. Edge," Laura said coldly. "I thought we could get better help and we were prepared to pay more dearly for it." She spat out a final two words: "Our mistake."

Blue Moon put his back to the tepee and stepped out on to the open area before the line of captive braves.

"You plan to do anything about it?"

"Like what?" Warren growled, staring with fascinated interest at Blue Moon and the prisoners as the chief's voice boomed out in his native tongue.

"Get the hell out of here. And warn Democracy about the threat from the reds—"

"Just like that?" Warren snarled, then lowered his tone as the chief finished saying his piece and there was silence outside. "Walk out, wave goodbye, and leave."

"Listen to the man, Dan," Laura urged. "You did what you had to last time he was around."

Edge grinned at her. "Nice I'm a good influence, ma'am."

She grimaced. "Is that what you are? Maybe you are, if it's only bad men who die whenever you're around."

She got that sightless glaze in her eyes again, as she stared out through the tepee entrance. Blue Moon had squatted on the ground and John Elk, looking suitably proud of how he was being rewarded for his capture of Edge, rose from among the watchers and stepped forward.

"Death's a lot older than me, ma'am," the half-breed said softly. "And he carried a bigger blade—up here."

He rested his hand on his shoulder, then delved under his coat collar and through the hair at the back of his head to draw the razor from its pouch. The woman ignored him but Warren licked his lips in eager anticipation.

"Time and place for everything, feller," Edge told him, folding the blade into the handle and clenching it in his fist as he thrust the hand into his pocket. "Just enjoy the show, and maybe pray."

Warren showed he was insulted, but was unable to tear his attention away from John Elk. Laura made it known she was aware of the exchange.

"Pray for what, Mr. Edge?"

"That these Indians are like most Indians."

"They are not stupid."

"Except when there's liquor around, ma'am. You just pray they got two bottle thirsts and one bottle heads."

Edge joined the Warrens then, in watching the scene outside. But nobody watched the young John Elk more closely than the five captives who were aware of their plight.

The castrated brave was tied to a pole at one end of the line, sagging against his bonds. John Elk snarled an order at him. When the command drew no response, he fisted a bunch of the injured brave's hair and jerked up his head. For a moment, the eyes in the pain-wracked face remained closed. But another snarl from Elk caused them to snap open. Elk took a knife from his weapon belt then and held it high, twisting it slowly so that the polished metal glinted in the red firelight.

The other five prisoners stared straight ahead, over the heads of the seated audience. Shouts of encouragement were yelled at Elk, between swigs from the bottles. The breathing of the men tied to the poles quickened. Sweat stood out on their faces and naked torsos. Pulses beat at the side of their throats.

Elk used his knife on the injured brave. There was no scream. Just some groans of disappointment from the watching Indians. Elk moved to the next prisoner in line

125

and the knife was used again. Then the next and the next. The groans died and the pace of the drinking increased. Low talk began, rising and falling, but the excitement heightened.

"The savages!" Dan Warren hissed between clenched teeth.

"It's their way, Dan," his wife countered, softly and absently. "We always knew it."

The man was staring at the line of prisoners with horror etched deeply into his fleshy face. The woman had the glazed look in her eyes.

Edge switched his attention lazily from the prisoners to the audience and back again. The glinting slits of his eyes and the relaxed set of his mouthline revealed nothing of what he thought about the scene.

"Mr. Edge?" Warren asked, unable to tear his gaze away from the evil on display beyond the tepee entrance. "Laura? Won't they listen to . . . can't we do somethin'? The chief and some of the others. . . ."

"No, Dan," his wife told him as John Elk returned to stand in front of the castrated brave. "We cannot do anything."

Warren shot a quick glance at Edge.

"They friends of yours, feller?" the half-breed asked.

"No, but . . ."

"So look on the bright side. If they were, you'd feel worse about it."

A roar of approval caused Warren to snap his head around and stare outside again.

John Elk had wrenched up the head of the injured brave again. There was blood on the prisoner's face, oozing from a long, shallow cut that ran from the corner of his left eye, down his cheek, across his chin, and up across the other cheek to the corner of the right eye.

The knife of the rewarded brave slashed twice, and if any sound of agony or terror was vented from the abruptly wide mouth of his victim, it was masked by the roar from the audience. Blood torrented from the face of the castrated brave. For a moment the head was held high, for all to see his agony, as the crimson gushed out of the deep wound, which followed precisely the line of the initial cut.

Then John Elk relinquished his grip on his first victim's hair and the head dropped forward. The vicious wounds were hidden, but the blood continued to flow, curtaining down the chest.

The second prisoner in the line had a shallow cut across his belly, from hip to hip. Aware of his fate, he sucked in his flesh, but the brave who stood before him made allowance for this. The knife swung from left to right, the blade slashing an inch-deep furrow. The lips of the wound opened wide and another torrent of blood erupted, to crawl across flesh and drip to the ground.

The audience of Sioux were howling and roaring their approval and encouragement in a continuous barrage of noise now.

The third prisoner was cut open from the base of the throat to the navel. The fourth was attacked at chest level, the wound he received almost a perfect circle, wide around his left nipple. The fifth felt the knife slicing into the flesh of his face, and spurted blood from ear to ear, along a line that took in his mouth—so that the lower halves of his cheeks flapped downwards to display his teeth amid the bubbling red froth.

The final prisoner suffered a slash across the forehead, then was cut open from the right shoulder to left hip.

John Elk had used the knife with great skill, digging in the point deep enough to cause a massive loss of blood without touching any vital organs.

The single word which he roared as he stepped away from the last prisoner in the line was not heard above the massed excitement of his audience. But somebody had been expecting it, and a buckskin bag was tossed at his feet. Broadening the grin of enjoyment he had displayed since the torture began, the young brave re-sheathed his knife and stooped to pick up the bag and open its neck.

"What else?" Dan Warren groaned. "They're gonna bleed to death anyway."

No one heard him.

John Elk, his hands, arms, and clothing drenched with the spurting blood of his victims, moved along the line again. And the shrill screams of agony from the throats of the helpless prisoners rose stridently above the noise of the watchers. For the young brave halted in front of each injured Indian, delved a hand into the bag, and, with calm deliberation, rubbed into their wounds a fist-ful of powdered rock salt.

Dan Warren covered his ears as the first brave screamed. He turned away when the second one added his anguish to the sound. He was vomiting a partially digested Sioux meal before the third shriek of agony was added to the cacophony. Then he collapsed into his own mess.

Elk completed his torture and the audience of Sioux was silenced by a raised hand gesture of Chief Blue Noon. The screams continued, less powerfully as the vocal chords of the suffering braves gave in to the strain.

"He's warning the rest of them." Laura Warren said dully as the chief began to boom out a speech, his words louder than the sounds of intense pain. "They will obey him or suffer a similar fate."

One by one, the braves doomed to die in agony lost the ability to give voice to their suffering. Blue Moon continued to address his warriors, lowering his tone as the competing sounds diminished.

"Now I guess he's telling them about the fine opportunity they have to strike a blow for the Indians against the whites," Edge muttered.

Laura sighed and turned away, to look sadly at her unconscious husband. "Yes. About how the whites are divided and when there is division, the enemy is at its weakest. Poor Dan."

The spilled contents of Warren's stomach were beginning to smell. His wife moved to him and struggled to turn him over onto his back. Then started to wipe the mess off his face with the hem of her dress. Edge shifted his blanket closer to the tepee entrance, spread it out, and lay down on it. He pushed his hat over his face.

Dan Warren returned to awareness. The chief completed his address and applause was thundered at him. Then the drinking began again. There was talk and laughter. Then the drums and chanting. The ground beneath Edge's blanket trembled with vibration from the feet which thudded the hard-packed mud in a war dance.

The Warrens talked softly. Laura was despondent at the outset. Gradually, her husband's voice lost its tone of determination and he became as miserable as she was. Edge stared into the darkness of the inside of his hat and fisted his hand loosely around the razor in his coat pocket.

Later, the Warrens became silent. Outside, the sounds of drunken merriment diminished. The prisoners sagged weakly against their bonds. The fire burned low. The cold of the night penetrated the Sioux encampment. The chill air neutralized the stink of death and dying, human waste and sickness, cheap liquor and burned tobacco.

Later still, Edge raised the brim of his hat. On the periphery of his vision, he saw the Warrens huddled together, staring at him. But he concentrated on the figure of John Elk. The young brave, his flesh and clothing crusted with congealed blood, was squatting at the entrance to the tepee, facing inwards. He was holding his Winchester, the hammer cocked.

"You have not been sleeping," the handsome young brave said. "Your mind works. Thinking of a way to escape. All this time wasted."

The hands of the brave tightened their grip on the rifle as Edge swung up into a sitting position, placing his hat back on his head. One-handed.

"Something else I should have been doing, feller?"

"Regretting that you were not born an Indian, White Eyes." He smiled. "But then, you would not have needed to try to do what you failed to do. Perhaps it is better if you sleep."

There was only the crackling of the fire and the movements of the horses in the rope corral to disturb the stillness of the camp now. The wind had dropped.

"John Elk speaks fine English, doesn't he?" Laura Warren said. "I taught him."

"What I learn, I learn well," the young brave boasted.

"Who taught you to torture?" Dan Warren snarled softly.

"My father," John Elk answered, smiling.

There was another series of sounds in addition to those from the fire and the horses. The deep breathing and muted snoring of the sleeping braves. Edge knew he had been hearing this for a long time but, once he accepted it, he ignored it. Until he was forced to consider again the possibility that other braves in addition to Elk had been ordered to stay sober. But he dismissed this along with all the other variables of the situation. Time was running out, which meant the time was right. He had no control over any actions or reactions except those he triggered within himself. It had been so ever since the proud young brave got the drop on him.

But even the man called Edge, stripped of so many failings and virtues accepted as a part of being a human

130

being, could not always keep doubts and wishful thoughts from interfering with the cool workings of his mind. He could only do his best to set them aside. And take risks calculated to the extent of his knowledge. In this instance, John Elk had to die. And whatever new dangers this invited was a decision in the hands of fate.

"He figured it was what you were cut out for?" Edge asked wryly.

"My father foresaw great things for his son, White Eyes. Soon all Sioux chiefs will be forced, like Blue Moon, to accept that I am destined to be a great warrior."

Dan Warren grimaced. His wife looked disappointed.

"You always said I was a fine pupil, Laura," John Elk recalled, still filled with pride.

Edge took his right hand out of his pocket. The folded razor was held along the palm and wrist, kept in place at one end between the two middle fingers. John Elk watched without suspicion as the half-breed cupped both hands in front of his mouth and blew on them.

Warren was still looking at the brave with unconcealed revulsion. But his wife saw Edge's actions and recalled seeing the razor earlier.

"That's right, John," she replied casually and sadly. "You were fine at your lessons. Many were, but you were always the star pupil. But it seems I did not teach any brave more than the language of the white man."

"For the White Eyes, it is a shame you did not realize this before you and your husband came here, Laura."

Edge used his teeth to half open the razor. Then bent his knees and pushed his elbows into his thighs. The woman did not look at him. She pretended a deep and melancholy interest in what the young brave was saying. John Elk glanced at the half-breed, but saw the movement as simply an attempt to combat the cold of night.

"Your father before me did not teach you about trust

131

and honor," the woman went on, recapturing Elk's attention.

"Yes!" he said, anger rising. "To my own people deserving of it."

The distance was four feet. Edge forced his feet back further, until the heels of his boots were hard against the backs of his thighs.

"You are not of my people. And those who are dying at my hand deserved the punishment. For they . . ."

Edge channeled every ounce of his strength to his feet and ankles. He leaned forward slightly, then powered into a forceful lunge.

John Elk turned his head.

Dan Warren gasped.

Laura did not alter her expression.

Edge reached forward with both hands, the right one making a flicking motion to swing the blade fully away from the handle of the razor.

The brave grunted and tracked the rifle on to the target. One of Edge's knees slammed against the barrel of the Winchester and forced the muzzle to the ground. Then his free hand was curled around the brave's neck. Terror was inscribed momentarily on the handsome young face. But training and the inbred knowledge of the Sioux came to the fore and his expression became set in hard lines. He was resigned to whatever the Great Spirits had in store for him.

The half-breed's right hand drove through the air on a slightly curved line. And the blade sank into the flesh of the Indian's throat. John Elk's Adam's apple bobbed once more. The accompanying sound was a muted gurgle, as expelled breath met flowing blood. His mouth fell open, much wider than his eyes. A crimson froth spilled over his lower lip. His hands held onto the rifle, a nerve spasm away from squeezing the trigger. But his heart stopped and the final response of his nervous system was to make his muscles go limp.

The new, still warm corpse started to fold. But Edge scrambled up onto his haunches and held the sagging body in a semblance of its former sitting posture. His glinting eyes stared out of their narrowed lids, seeking a sign of danger. Menace was latent beyond the dark entrance of every tepee. But no alarm was raised.

"Holy cow!" Warren hissed. "That was incredible."

"The kid said he learned fast," the half-breed muttered, allowing the body to fold to the ground. "One lesson and he died real good."

"I meant . . ."

"He knows what you meant, Dan," Laura cut in, all traces of her trancelike state missing now. "What next, Mr. Edge?"

The razor had come clear of the flesh as the corpse slid into a heap on the ground. Edge wiped the blood from the blade on the back of Elk's shirt and replaced it in the pouch. Then he jerked the rifle out from under the dead weight.

"You've got a choice, ma'am," he replied, moving to the rear of the tepee and going out full-length on the dirt. "Fighting them here on your own. Or making a try for town where there'll be help."

"You think we can make it back to Democracy, Edge?" Warren asked.

"What can we do here?" his wife answered tensely, moving to follow Edge.

"Kill the braves one by one and hope none of them scream," the half-breed offered as Warren remained seated, shaking his head. "Or maybe set light to the wagons and pray the booze keeps everyone asleep until the shells explode."

He lifted the bottom of the tepee canvas and bellied outside. He was in a squat, having made a survey of the

133

encampment and its surroundings, when Laura Warren slid out into the open. Her husband was only a moment behind her.

"We're with you, Edge," Dan whispered, glancing fearfully around. "On our own, we ain't done nothin' right."

"Yeah," the half-breed growled. "And you ought to carry a quarantine flag. It's catching."

"What do . . ." Laura started to say.

"Just do what I do," Edge interrupted. "There ain't no sugar to make things easier to swallow. And there sure ain't no guarantee that it'll keep what ails us from being fatal."

"Okay," Dan said.

"All right," Laura augmented.

Edge dropped forward on to his hands and knees and started away from the tepee, heading initially for the cover of the horses in the rope corral. Laura stayed close behind him and Dan brought up the rear. The half-breed spent as much time looking away from the ring of tepees as toward it: aware that boredom, resentment, and jealousy might cause the sentries to cast frequent glances back toward the braves who had been allowed to enjoy the revels before the battle to come.

But the three escapers made the relative safety of the corral without an alarm being raised. The Warrens had built up a resistance to sudden death and its aftermath by now. Thus, when they saw the now cleansed corpse of Fay Reeves slumped in the middle of the stream, her eyes staring sightlessly at them as her hair billowed to the tug of the current, they neither showed nor uttered any sign of horror. Just as they could look back at the now dead braves tied to the tepee poles and perhaps think, just as Edge did, only that the Indians were six who were no threat.

The half-breed halted only for a few moments, to

glance in every direction. Then he moved out into the icy water, still crawling but using just one hand. The other held the rifle in the dry. The noise of the crossing added little to the constant rippling and bubbling of the water over its uneven rock bed. There was no pause on the far bank. Instead, Edge went out full-length and bellied on a parallel course to the water, until he reached the end of the grade with the bluff beyond it.

The Warrens were grateful for the respite, rubbing their faces and hugging themselves. But this had little effect on the bone-deep cold of the night, aggravated by clothing sodden with icy water.

"If the Indians don't get us, we could freeze to death," the woman muttered through chattering teeth.

Just as he did back at the abandoned way station when the situation was at its most critical, Dan Warren became the dominant partner again. "If we'd stayed in the tepee, been only one way," he pointed out.

Edge ignored them, as the man put an arm around the shoulders of his wife to try to impart some strength of will rather than body heat. The half-breed scanned the country to the south and the west, seeking to pinpoint the position of the sentries. There were no longer any sound clues, for ever since the Sioux camp had erupted with noise at the conclusion of the council, the birdcall signals had been curtailed.

He saw three shadowy forms to the south and chose to ignore them. Because they were positioned far enough out to be beyond earshot of any noise Edge intended to make.

"Stay put," he said at length, placing the Winchester on the ground. "And be ready to move fast. Bring this."

Laura was set to ask a question, but Edge was already moving: erect but in the deep moon shadow of the bluff. There were eight sentries watching the western approach to the campsite. For cover, they were using rocks, brush, and small hollows. With the bluff between themselves and the camp, they had no reason to look behind them. Unless a noise aroused their suspicion—and the half-breed put his feet to the ground as silently as a stalking animal closing in for the kill.

The braves were positioned at intervals of about twenty yards, hidden from an enemy in front of them. But vulnerable from the rear.

The moon was as bright as it had ever been that night. Any eye looking in the right direction would have seen Edge clearly as he left the cover of the bluff shadow and approached a patch of brush. He was on his hands and knees again. But instead of the Winchester he was holding the razor ready opened.

The brave was sitting cross-legged, a blanket draped around him, absently picking his nose as he peered through the brush at the empty landscape. He was just about to eat what his probing finger had found when the brown-skinned fist appeared in front of his face. He started to snap his head around, but his eyes had traveled only as far as the crook of the half-breed's elbow when the fist was jerked sideways. The blade of the razor slit the throat neatly, from one side to the other. And Edge's other hand slammed over the gaping mouth to trap a possible scream inside.

"Feeding time's over, feller," Edge drawled softly, as he wiped the razor blade clean of more blood and drew the brave's knife from its sheath. "Pretty soon your belly'll know your throat's been cut."

He put the razor back in the sheath and approached the second sentry on all fours again, curving out and then in, to make his attack from the rear. It was simple. The brave was asleep, sprawled out on his back under a blanket. A rifle was close at hand, but had rolled out of the palm. Edge rose up onto his knees, and brought both hands down at once. The right buried the knife blade to the hilt in the chest of the sleeping Indian, left of center. The other clamped over the mouth to cut off a dying sound.

"Asleep is the best way to go," the half-breed rasped, his lips curled back and his teeth clenched in a grin of ice-cold evil.

He was a long way from finishing what he had started and correcting the error which had led him into becoming involved with the troubles of Democracy. But the process of restitution was underway. The greed-blinded citizens of the town, apathetic to everything except their own selfishness, might yet be saved from the worst kind of trouble.

But the half-breed did not even think about the town and the people in it as he plunged the knife into the vulnerable flesh of two more unsuspecting Sioux braves. In the act of cold-bloodedly killing the enemy, he was concerned solely with the survive-or-perish aspect of the moment.

That was another lesson of war which had served him well, in uniform and out of it. The overall strategy, the wider implications, were immaterial when one man faced another in mortal combat.

When he had first learned this lesson—to concentrate mentally and physically on the immediate kill-or-be-killed situation—he had relished the knowledge. Had reveled in his ability to survive. Indeed, he had fought his first full-scale battles in a kind of euphoric exhilaration. But that had passed. For he had come to take his killing skills for granted. And the taut-faced grin he now displayed at the moment of killing was an expression of triumph. An officer of higher rank, a man who hired him to do a job, or his own decision to follow a course of action: whatever or whoever it was put his life on the line, had no place in his mind as he defended that life.

137

He did what was necessary, accepted the result with a grin, and moved to the next confrontation.

A brave stood up and whirled, reacting to the crack of a bone. There was a rifle in the Indian's hands, but neither the muzzle nor the brave's eyes sought out the approaching half-breed.

The brave grunted and pumped the lever action of the Winchester. Edge pushed himself up onto his haunches, drew back his right arm, then threw it forward. The knife spun in the cold air.

Moonlight glinted on another blade turning end over end.

Edge's knife sank deep into the Indian's neck, just beneath the ear. The second blade buried itself in the brave's heart. The groan might have become a strident scream of terror, agony, or warning. But there was not time. The Indian died with his mouth gaping wide. He dropped the rifle, staggered backwards, hit the rocks which had been his cover, and collapsed in front of them.

"That John Elk ain't the only son ever learned things from his old man," Dan Warren growled, rising from a clump of brush. "Kinda rusty on some thin's. But I'm brushin' up fast."

The fleshy, dirt-streaked, heavily bristled face of the rancher showed a grin of its own.

"The other three?" Edge asked.

"Stalkin' whatever kinda game they have up in the happy huntin' ground," Warren reported happily, as he stooped to claim the dead brave's discarded rifle. "Buffalo with wings I reckon."

"So that's where they've gone," the half-breed growled.

"Took Elk's knife before we left the tepee. Came in real useful. Easier than slaughterin' beef."

"Don't boast, Dan," Laura said, emerging from out of

138

the shadow of the bluff. She extended the Winchester toward Edge. "Pride led to the downfall of John Elk."

Warren replaced the grin with a scowl and nodded toward Edge. "At least he could say thanks for the help I give him."

The half-breed was temporarily out of danger. He didn't have to think about killing and there was room in his mind to consider why it had been necessary to kill, and would probably be necessary to kill again.

"Edge didn't ask you to help," Laura pointed out quickly. "At the start of it, it was the other way around."

The husband and wife both looked at the half-breed expectantly. Obviously hoping to get a more precise reason for his involvement than he had given back at the tepee. But, if he had an answer for their steady gazes and the question they posed, it was too complex to explain in the cold of a predawn hour close to an encampment of hostile Sioux Indians.

"Was it the money, Edge?" Dan blurted out suddenly.

Laura rested a restraining hand on his arm. Then cocked her head on one side, looking harder at the tall, lean half-breed, and sighed. "If we live through this," she said, "will we talk about our part in starting it to the others?"

"Guess not," her husband allowed, bewildered.

Laura nodded. "Precisely. No one likes admitting their mistakes."

"Sure, Laura. But it's only human to make them."

"And divine to forgive," the woman said softly. "As the old proverb goes. But to forgive oneself . . . that can be the hardest thing of all. Is that not so, Mr. Edge?"

"That's too damn deep for me!" her husband growled. "All I know is that we should get the hell outta here before them Indians wake outta their drunk sleeps."

"But it makes sense to you, Mr. Edge?" Laura Warren insisted.

"Could be, ma'am," Edge allowed, and touched the brim of his hat in acknowledgement. "But I figure your husband ain't exactly talking out of the back of his head."

"Just anxious not to get a hole in it—or anyplace else."

"I'm sorry we got you into this!" Laura called as Edge started around the heap of rocks.

"No sweat, lady," the half-breed rasped. "If I figured it was your fault, you'd have known before now."

"Hey, that sounds like he meant he'd have . . ."

"Shut up, Dan!" Laura cut in, and gave him a shove in the wake of the departing Edge. "If he wasn't the way he is, perhaps neither of us would be here now."

With all the sentries on the west of the camp dead, the trio made good time to the stand of timber where the tethered horses and the hog-tied Conrad Power had been forced to wait.

"Edge, that you?" the pained and frightened voice of the Negro called as he heard the footfalls of the two men and woman coming close.

"Guess you could say that," the half-breed answered cryptically, drawing the razor from its pouch as he approached the bound man and stooped at his side.

Power shot a surprised look at the Warrens, then glared at Edge. "Could be better for you if you get my shotgun outta reach before you untie me, mister," he warned. "I been workin' up a lotta hate for you while you been gone."

"Didn't expect a warm welcome," Edge answered, stepping back and watching as the black man got unsteadily to his feet. Power stamped his feet and massaged his wrists, to get the circulation restarted and to warm himself.

The Warrens were more surprised to see Power than he was at their presence.

"You were better off here, Conrad, believe me," Dan

Warren assured him. "The Sioux are fixin' to hit town on their own account. Laura and me, we made one big mistake."

For a few moments, the handsome black face continued to express cold-pinched disgust. But it was all directed toward the Warrens. When he snapped his head around to watch the half-breed swinging up into the saddle of the mare, there was a mixture of fear and helplessness in his features.

"Ain't there anythin' we can do, mister?" he pleaded.

"Head for town before the Sioux win it, feller. Election or not. And I guess we don't need to take no opinion poll to decide it had better be at a gallop."

Chapter Eleven

THEY rode tandem, Laura up behind Edge and her husband on the Negro's gelding to distribute the weight evenly between the two horses. But the animals suffered anyway from the additional load and the pace at which they were ridden.

At first the horses and riders welcomed the speed which set the blood racing through their veins to create body heat. Inevitably, though, as dawn spread a dull grey light across the sky from the east, weariness and the threat of exhaustion to the horses became a greater discomfort than the cold.

So, as the gap between the escapers and the Sioux camp widened, rest periods were called more often. Sometimes they were actual halts. More often the riders dismounted and walked for several hundred yards, leading the mare and the gelding by the reins.

During the initial respites from the frenetic race against time, Dan and Laura Warren tried to convey the extent of their remorse to the Negro. But Power was indifferent to them. He made it plain, with snarling words, that his sole concern for the moment was to get to Democracy before the Sioux.

Edge never spoke at all. It was he who set the pace, called the rest periods, and indicated when they were over. And the others accepted his command by following his examples.

They rode or walked the horses along the old stage trail, between the derelict farmsteads, and then, past the abandoned way station, swung on to the Laramie-Democracy trail. When they were beyond the halfway point—further from the camp than town—the Warrens and Power began to show more anxious interest in what lay ahead than looking for the threat that was behind them. The half-breed continued to scan the terrain on every side with narrowed eyes whose glinting intensity was the only clue to the extent of his watchfulness in a bristled face which otherwise looked relaxed.

The sky was blue now, the sun a perfect sphere of bright yellow above the distant horizon. But the air felt as cold as it had been at the darkest hour of the night. Nothing was moving on the vast landscape, except the two horses and four riders, when Democracy came in sight. The chiming of the town clock, marking the hour of nine, seemed this morning to have the tone of a death knell.

Dark pillars of smoke stood up from many chimneys above the town. But the quartet had to ride much closer before they could smell the burning wood. And by that time they could see the people. Men and women in a large group gathered on the intersection: and men positioned on rooftops tracking the approach of the newcomers with rifles.

Everyone was dressed warmly, their breath misting as it was expelled. News that four riders astride two horses were approaching town had been spread and every pair of eyes in Democracy was turned toward the slow-moving group.

Laura tightened her grip around the waist of Edge.

"We oughta yell," Power rasped. "They'll likely just start blastin' at us."

143

As he spoke the final word, a rifle shot cracked out. A divot of dirt was dug from the mud, six feet in front of the two horses. Both animals were too weary to do anything but snort and toss their heads at the abrupt disturbance.

"Kerwin, we said to let them through!" the familiar voice of Sheriff Stanton roared from out of the crowd on the intersection.

Edge and Power had both reined in their horses. But neither made a move to reach for the Winchester or shotgun. Up on the roofs of the business premises lining the north section of Main Street, the Kerwin gang maintained a steady aim with their rifles. Gun barrels and the five-pointed stars pinned to their chests glinted in the morning sunlight.

"No trouble, you don't make it," a man called down in a voice thick with a Southern drawl. "Just need your attention for a while."

"That's Nathan Kerwin," Power whispered from the side of his mouth. "Cass on his right and Tim the other side."

"You fellers are hard to ignore," Edge called back to Nate Kerwin and his brothers, who were standing on the flat roof of the Democracy Bank, across the street from the law office.

"So's a fat whore name of Fay Reeves, mister. If you ever see her. You seen her since she left this town?"

None of the brothers was tall. Nate was the tallest. And the oldest. About thirty-five. Tim was a year or so younger. Cass was still in his midtwenties. All were stockily built with faces which bore a family resemblance. Over a distance, they were quite good looking.

Edge jerked a thumb over his shoulder. "Place called Whitehead Crossing."

Nate grinned. His brothers and some of the other

hired guns on different rooftops grimaced their dislike of the information.

"Whorin'?"

"Dead."

Anger replaced the grin on Nate's face and suddenly he looked ugly. Elsewhere on the rooftops there was relief.

"How?"

"The Sioux," Edge answered, sensing Power staring at his profile in awe. Nobody had told the Negro about the death of Fay Reeves. "She didn't die easy."

The news took some of the fire out of the gunman's anger. "Just for the hell of it, mister?"

Edge shook his head. "A brave thought he could have her for free. She castrated him. Should have cut off his legs instead. He was still man enough to catch her."

Nate turned his face to the bright blue sky. And vented a harsh roar of laughter. "Always said it about that bitch. She had balls."

During the exchange, Edge had divided his attention between the men on the roof and the crowd at the intersection. The entire population of Democracy, with the exception of children, seemed to be gathered in front of the Palace Hotel. Before the newcomers rode into sight of town, a raised wooden platform before the hotel porch had been the center of attention. The platform was long and broad enough to accommodate a dozen chairs and a table. A brightly painted banner was hung above the platform, supported by a pole at each end. Every chair beneath the banner had been occupied. But now the men were standing, leaning forward over the table to peer along the north section of Main Street.

Gene Stanton had been one of those on the platform. But he had climbed down hurriedly when the shot exploded—and the crowd had parted to allow him through. He stood now, in isolation, at the point where the street

145

ran between the town meeting hall and the stage line depot to enter the intersection. His long coat was unbuttoned and his right hand draped over the ornate butt of his Beaumont-Adams revolver.

"Let them through!" he yelled. "But keep them covered!"

Nate Kerwin gestured with his Winchester. "It's us and our boys he's payin'. But I guess you better follow his orders, too, uh?"

"And remember," Tim warned. "No trouble from you and no trouble from us."

"We'll be watchin' you," the young Cass added.

Edge jerked his thumb over his shoulder again as he heeled his mare forward. "Couple of you fellers better watch that way," he advised as Power moved the gelding to follow him.

"The Sioux are fixin' to attack!" Dan Warren added, his voice croaky.

Every rooftop gunman snapped his head around to peer into the north. And there was a grimace back on every face.

"He didn't say we'd have to fight Injuns, Nate!" Tim complained.

"Gotta be a higher rate for that job," the eldest brother growled as the four riders on two horses moved slowly past the bank.

"You hear that, Frank?" Stanton called, his voice raised to be heard above the swell of nervous talk. "The Sioux are stirred up!"

The obese Frank Snyder was in the place of honor at the center of the row of politicians on the platform. He said something to those on either side of him and they resumed their seats with reluctance, all but one craning forward to try to look along Main Street—beyond the approaching riders and the men on the rooftops and out across open country. The exception was the school-

146

teacher, Tillson, who was more afraid of something already in town.

"People of Democracy!" Snyder roared, throwing his hands high in the air, a broad smile on his pale, fleshy features. "This morning you have been to the polls and by your unanimous vote put your faith in me and what I stand for!"

The tall and thin Stanton was still standing with a hand draped over his gun butt. His dead-looking eyes never wandered from the newcomers as the horses were angled to the hitching rail outside the stage line depot and the riders began to dismount.

"You were stupid to come back here," the elderly lawman accused. "If you try to reach that rifle and shotgun you'll fine out quick just how stupid."

Neither the half-breed nor the Negro had attempted to touch their weapons.

"Mr. Stanton!" Laura said urgently. "The Sioux. We have to get ready to . . ."

"We've delivered the message," her husband cut in sourly. "What we came back here to do."

"And to be hanged," Stanton reminded, curling back his lips in a scowling grin.

"Having done that," Snyder continued, speaking to a now quiet audience and talking above the exchange between Stanton and the newcomers, "I ask you to show that faith. The sheriff has a fine band of able deputies. They have already warned us that one group of enemies of Democracy were approaching. And have spiked their guns, as it were. They are in a position to give us ample warning of any new threat. And we will be prepared . . ."

The elderly, sandy-haired Jethro Lovejoy was up on the platform. So was the stout Maggie Woodward. Silas McQuigg, a white patch on his forehead, his partner Harry Grant, and the rat-faced Jay Bailey. The mortician, Meek, and the Reverend Flint. Young, the town druggist, Thomas Waters who ran the newspaper, and Swan, the banker. The old mayor and town councillors showing that they had joined forces with those newly elected to the offices. All of them neatly dressed in fine clothes.

"Frank is my name and honest is my character!" the new mayor went on. "Frank and Honest Snyder! Who won your confidence by promising fair shares for all in Democracy! Equal rights and equal wealth!"

Edge had rolled a cigarette and was smoking it, seemingly detached from all that was going on about him. The Warrens were peering anxiously northwards. Conrad Power scowled at the boasting figure standing on the platform.

"Seems like some of them coyotes are more equal than others," the Negro growled, looking along the row of finely clad figures, then eyeing the big audience, all of them dressed ready for work. "Look at them . . . like animals. Friggin' sheep!" He spat at the ground. "But greedy as pigs."

"Shut your mouth, nigger!" Stanton ordered.

"That sounds like a farmful of animals, Conrad," Edge muttered.

"You shut up, too!" Stanton snarled, fisting his hand around the gun butt.

"What'll you do, watchful big brother?" the Negro challenged.

"Shut all your mouths!" Stanton half drew the Beaumont-Adams. "Or we'll . . ."

"Kill those who are already condemned to death?" Laura Warren posed, still looking for the first sign of the Indian attack.

"For the first time since this town was built, the people are going to own it!" Snyder shouted, warming to his subject. "It's going to be just what this banner proclaims!"

He half turned and gestured with a hand to the sign strung above the platform.

"Big wheels!" Power muttered venomously. "They make me sick!"

Edge dropped his cigarette and crushed out the fire under a heel. "Seems they also make big revolutions, feller," he muttered.

The grin on Snyder's face as he turned fully towards his audience again became an evil smirk.

"Friends!" he roared, adding stridency to his voice as anxiety about the threat of a Sioux attack took a firmer hold over the gathering. "Comrades! Most of those who at first opposed the will of the people have been won over. Some have not. Up here on this platform is a man who refuses to stand aside from the path of progress."

He half turned again, but looked down instead of up. At the slightly built Tillson seated immediately to his left. He dropped a hand to cup the bony shoulder of the schoolteacher.

"This man! A man with whom we entrusted the education of our children. Who has shown himself to be an enemy unwilling to accept the offer of friendship from the majority."

The fat Snyder had recaptured the attention of his audience. And there was a tense expectancy emanating from the crowd during an interlude of silence in which Snyder tightened his grip on Tillson's shoulder and forced the man to his feet.

The schoolteacher was unshaven and shabby. Perhaps fear had stamped the haggard look on his thin face. Or perhaps it was the result of his experiences since he had surrendered to the lawman on the roof of the stage line depot.

Still holding the man's shoulder, Snyder used his other

149

hand to turn Tillson's head and force it around and upwards—to direct the eyes at the vividly painted banner.

"Read it!" the new mayor ordered. "Loud, for everyone to hear."

Tillson looked wretchedly defeated. But his voice was loud in the taut silence. "No."

Snyder injected more evil into his grin as he released his hold on the man. He reached under his expensively tailored suit jacket and drew out a tiny under-and-over Derringer. Lovejoy and the Reverend Flint half rose, ready to protest. But then, as the twin barrels of the small gun were pressed against the side of Tillson's head, they realized the futility of what they planned.

"Read it, or I'll kill you!" Snyder rasped.

Every eye was directed toward the two men standing at the center of the platform. The menace of a potential Indian attack was temporarily forgotten as a more imminent threat of sudden death presented itself. Even the Kerwin gang on the rooftops, and the Warrens, found their attention drawn toward Snyder and Tillson.

"I mean it, mister! One last chance! Read it or die!"

There was a moment of silence. Beads of sweat could be seen on the faces of the threatened man and the one who posed the threat.

Tillson's throat worked. "No, damn you!"

Snyder's smirk became a scowl and he squeezed a trigger. A single bullet crashed through the side of Tillson's skull, behind his right ear. The charge was not powerful enough to drive the shell completely through his head. But it reached his brain and he died on his feet, then corkscrewed to the platform. The report from the small caliber gun was just a scratch on the silence. The crash as the crumpling body knocked over a chair was much louder.

"So will we purge ourselves of all who dare to stand

in our way!" Snyder thundered, silencing the first mumblings of vocal shock. He waved the tiny gun to indicate the sign again, but did not have to turn to read the luridly painted words. "And it is your way. Because you voted my ticket. The right way. For, as our banner proudly proclaims: *This is Now The People's Democracy!*"

"That poor Mr. Tillson!" Laura blurted out tearfully, as Snyder glowered his rage at receiving only a smattering of applause—most of it from those on the platform. "What a stupid reason to die!"

Edge pursed his lips. "Guess he figured better dead than read, ma'am."

Then Cass Kerwin's voice robbed Snyder of his audience. With a single word, bellowed loud: "Indians!"

Chapter Twelve

THE two ridden-out horses snorted and reared against their tethers as Edge whirled and lunged between them. With one hand he drew the Winchester from the boot on the mare and the other snatched at the shotgun hung from the saddlehorn on the gelding.

"Edge!" Power snapped.

The half-breed turned and saw that Stanton had his revolver out and aimed. The dead eyes were as dangerous as the black muzzle of the Beaumont-Adams.

"The people in this town been warned about pointing guns at me, feller," Edge said, loud above the barrage of noise which Kerwin's warning had triggered. "But I figure personal business can wait awhile?"

The victory rally of Snyder and his fellow politicians was totally disrupted. He and some of the others on the platform attempted to bring back order, but it was useless. People were racing away from the intersection in every direction, panic in their haste, their expressions, and their voices. Then, when some of his colleagues scrambled to the ground, calling for their wives and children, Snyder admitted defeat.

And there was fear on his face as he forced his way through the scattering crowd toward Stanton. The three Kerwin brothers, who approached the sheriff from another direction, were cool and calm.

"Gene!" Snyder shrieked. "You'd better give everyone his gun back. We're gonna need every . . ."

"You figure you need us, mister?" Nate Kerwin cut in.

Suddenly, there was indecision in the lawman's eyes. His stars wavered, but his gun stayed pointed at Edge.

"Indians weren't part of the deal," Tim Kerwin added. "Nate and us figure double what we been given."

"We'll pay, we'll pay!" Snyder agreed, licking sweat from his lips and mopping it from his forehead as he peered fearfully along the north stretch of Main Street. "Anything you want. Take it. The guns, Gene. Give people back their . . ."

"What about the prisoners?" Stanton interrupted.

"Where they gonna escape to?" Nate Kerwin growled. "And you people need every gun hand you got."

"Right, right!" Snyder concurred, more agitated by the second. "Let's move. We have to organize."

Stanton fixed his dead eyes on Edge. "You'll keep, stranger!" he snarled.

The half-breed nodded. "Best way to keep anything is put it on ice, feller."

The lawman thrust the revolver back into his holster and broke into a run toward his office. Snyder waddled in his wake, yelling out for men to follow and get their guns. Dan Warren, steering his wife with him, was among the first to comply.

Edge tossed the shotgun to Power, who caught it and then delved into a saddlebag for extra shells.

"You guys!" the eldest Kerwin called as the half-breed and the Negro started across the intersection toward the hotel. "Me and the boys've got scores to settle with you. After."

"Didn't expect nothin' else, mister," Power yelled back.

"Over to the right!" a man up on the roof of the

153

church roared. "The red bastards are comin' in from the right!"

"But that sure is a twist," Edge growled, breaking into a run and leaping up onto the sidewalk to push through the batswing doors into the saloon.

He led the way, Power trailing, into the lobby and up the stairway. Then through his old room, out of the broken window, and onto the sidewalk roof. He tossed the Winchester up onto the roof of the hotel and hauled himself after it.

Below, the streets were rapidly emptying, men running into the law office and then emerging with guns. All over town, figures appeared on roofs to reinforce the Kerwin gang already in position at high points. Other defenders crouched behind windows and in doorways.

"We should've made them listen!" Power snarled. "We should've shouted down that fat slob and made them get ready for this! They're every which where, Edge! Ain't nobody in charge and . . ."

"Warren told them, feller," Edge answered evenly, pumping the action of the Winchester as he looked across the town toward the advancing Indians. "But it seems the people of Democracy only listen to what they want to hear—until it's too late."

It was not only the effects of too much liquor which had delayed the Sioux. They had held back at Whitehead Crossing for a stronger reason.

Reinforcements.

There had been less than fifty Indians at the camp when Edge and the Warrens made their escape. Some of them squaws. There were more than double that number now, all warriors—all wearing feathered war bonnets and with paint daubed on their faces.

They advanced slowly, holding their ponies to a walk. Their rifle barrels glinted in the morning sunlight. So did the tips of the lances some of them carried. But arrowheads were covered where they protruded from the pouches—by balls of rag tied in place.

The Sioux moved toward their target from the northeast, in five rows twenty braves wide. Chief Blue Moon rode slightly ahead of the first row, at the center.

The town, its streets now totally deserted, became as silent as the advance of the war band.

The braves rode erect on the backs of their ponies.

Men on the roofs of the town buildings and in the doorways and windows crouched lower.

"You see the Kerwin brothers any place, Conrad?" Edge asked.

"Frig them!" the Negro muttered. "Enough I can see the friggin' Indians."

"The bastards!" Gene Stanton roared into the silence. "It's the Warrens' doin'! Them Injuns are the help the bastard and his wife went to get!"

"He thinks slower than you do," Power said. "Sure hope he's as rusty on the draw as he says."

The sheriff's enraged voicing of his realization drew a response of more angry words—swelling in volume as the revelation was spread throughout the frightened town.

"Sure hope Dan and Laura are someplace safe," the Negro rasped.

Blue Moon thrust a hand high above his head.

"Like to know where it is," Edge answered.

The chief's hand fell forward. Heels thudded into horse flesh and the thunder of unshod hooves against hard-packed dirt was almost masked by howling war whoops from massed throats.

The anger of the townspeople was directed away from the Warrens toward the advancing Sioux.

The galloping riders crossed into effective rifle range and a barrage of gunfire exploded. Cordite smoke drifted above the town and trailed out behind the attackers.

Edge and Power both went out full-length on their bellies, canting their guns over the lip of the hotel roof. They held their fire.

But others traded bullets with the attackers. Braves were flung from ponies, pumping blood from their wounds. Or ponies were hit and spilled their riders beneath the hooves of other ponies.

Sioux shells shattered windows, splintered timber, or pocked brickwork. Some found flesh and the defenders of Democracy suffered their first casualties.

"Hey!" Power yelled in delight. "The stupid bastards have come to their senses. We're murderin' them. They're standin' up for themselves and we're slaughterin' them redskins. They must still be drunk or somethin'!"

Elsewhere, on rooftops and at street level, the tone of the shouting changed from fear to glee. For anyone who had a clear view of what was happening could see the Sioux were losing at least three braves to every one white man who was hit.

Edge remained silent. In the law office, Stanton also held his peace. The members of the Kerwin gang on the roofs concentrated on picking off the attackers without voicing their thoughts. But all these men, experienced in gun battles of one sort or another, realized that the full frontal assault on the town was just one aspect of the Sioux's strategy.

And this was proved as the front runners of the Indian attack reached the cover of the buildings. For they, and most of the braves behind them, skidded their ponies to a rearing halt and leapt to the ground.

Painted and feathered figures, inert and writhing, featured the final stretch of the Sioux advance on the town. For those who had been hit by flesh-tearing lead, it had been a suicidal assault. And others continued to invite certain death—staying astride their ponies to gallop flat out along the street, firing into the buildings on either side. Some hit nothing but blank walls before bullets from the defenders' guns knocked their bleeding bodies to the ground. Others took life before giving up their own.

One war-whooping brave got as far as the intersection, and was knocked into a backward somersault from his horse. It was a shell from Edge's Winchester which had exploded pulp and bone splinters from the Indian's skull.

The Indian died with a triumphant war cry on his lips. Sacrificing his life in the same altruistic manner as those who had already fallen: dying in the way every Indian warrior dreamed of. Honorably, on the field of battle with a hated enemy.

But others still lived. On the ground and out of sight in the cover of the buildings as the second stage of the Sioux attack was put into action.

"This friggin' thing's no damn good at this range!" Power snarled, banging the twin barrels of his shotgun against the roof.

"Don't knock it until you get a chance to try it, Conrad," the half-breed advised, nodding along the north section of Main Street.

It was crowded with riderless ponies, some halted, some rearing and scratching at the ground, some still galloping flat out. The Negro looked, and saw that the only braves in sight were either sprawled in bullet-riddled death or struggling to drag their pain-wracked bodies into cover. Rifle and revolver fire cracked out and the wounded spurted more blood and became still. Other guns exploded from other sources and the killers of the wounded were hit.

"How many made it, you reckon?" Power asked.

"It matter, feller?"

"Enough of them," Power groaned.

157

"So it matters, Conrad. Enough of them to finish this town if somebody doesn't take command."

A hail of fire arrows was arced high and long across the roofs. They emerged from billowing black smoke already rising from buildings on either side at the end of Main Street.

"You got what it takes, Edge," Power yelled, watching as some arrows fell harmlessly to the ground, while others thudded into timber walls and roofs.

"I had what it took to warn these people, feller. It ain't my town."

Smoke began to wisp up from other buildings on Main Street, as evidence of the attackers' progress deeper into town. Most of the rooftops were deserted of men now. Except for those who could not come down: lay dead or dying as they waited to be incinerated.

Another volley of fire arrows hissed through the smoke. Two of the street-hung banners were set alight by fire arrows. The canvas burned fiercely and the supporting ropes snapped. The banners whooshed down towards the fronts of buildings and the flames roared more violently as they fed on timber.

Men, women, and children rushed out onto the street from burning buildings and raced through the smoke. Arrows and bullets hissed and cracked toward them to pierce and tear their flesh.

"What can I do, Edge?" Power screamed, his eyes glistening with tears as he stared in horror at slumped, blood-run corpses piled on the street.

"Fight them on their own level," the half-breed answered, sliding over the lip of the roof, then leaping down off the sidewalk porch. "Before they light a fire under you."

Bullets cracked either side of him. He fired into the acrid smoke, pumped the rifle's action, and fired again. Then he whirled, as the Negro leapt off the roof and hit

158

the ground beside him. Power was unbalanced as he landed and went over heavily onto his side.

A brave came racing out through the batswing doors of the saloon, a tomahawk raised to throw. His target was the cursing black man. Edge squeezed the rifle trigger. The Indian took the bullet in the throat and was slammed back through the doors.

"One score settled, Conrad," the half-breed yelled, leaping up onto the sidewalk and flattening himself against the wall.

Smoke wafted out through the doors and two more braves charged from the saloon with it. Both had rifles.

Edge shot the first one through the side of the head. Power was on his feet then, in a half crouch. One barrel of the shotgun belched spraying death. The front of the brave's torso was suddenly a moving mass of bright crimson, his rib cage gleaming white through the blood.

"I ain't the only feller around here to get something off his chest," Edge muttered as the Indian fell back through the smoke.

"They're puttin' the whole town to the torch!" a man shrieked from the stage line depot.

"My place!" Power groaned, and there were more tears in his eyes as he gazed at the smoke billowing from the saloon and the flickering flames at the windows. "The bastards have got to my place!"

The Sioux had infiltrated deep into Democracy. Buildings on the north stretch of Main Street and both lengths of the cross street were blazing. The defenders were in panicked retreat.

"There they go!" Frank Snyder bellowed across the crackling flames and crack of gunfire. "It's them that caused it!"

The fat man came running out of the meeting hall, the tiny Derringer in his hand. His arm was stretched out in front of him and a tiny spurt of flame showed momentarily at the upper muzzle.

Dan and Laura Warren were at the head of a group of fleeing people. They were all running fast. Not chasing the Warrens: the only thought in their minds to escape from the relentless pursuit of the war-whooping Sioux.

The bullet hit Laura in the leg and she was pitched out of her run. She hit the ground with a scream. Her husband stooped at her side. In what was literally blind panic, the terrified crowd behind the couple did not waver from their course. They charged into the Warrens, stumbling, picking themselves up, and staggering on again.

They raced onto the south section of Main Street, which was the only area still clear of smoke, flames, and crumpled corpses.

A flying boot had hit Dan Warren in the face. He was sprawled in unmoving unconsciousness and Laura, one leg useless, was trying to shake him back to awareness.

"You sonofabitch!" Power screamed, swinging his shotgun, his face a black mask of intense hatred.

"You ain't got enough gun, feller," Edge warned.

The Negro's finger was tight on the trigger.

Then a fire arrow streaked across the intersection. Snyder had half turned to race away from the menace of the shotgun. The arrow thudded into his hip and his expensive suit jacket burst into flames as he screamed.

"Help me!" he pleaded. He turned again, and lunged toward Edge and Power. The flames engulfed his entire upper body and set fire to his hair.

"Moves fast for such a fat man, don't he?" the Negro snarled.

"He's traveling light," Edge answered.

Power squeezed the trigger. Snyder's head exploded in a gruesome mess of blood and bone fragments.

"He just lost some more ugly fat," Power growled, breaking open the gun and ejecting the empty cartridges as the almost headless corpse dropped to the ground and the gushing blood extinguished the flames.

"Help me!" Laura Warren pleaded.

She was half upright, dragging her injured leg and the unresponsive form of her husband. Anguish showed through the hair plastered to her soot-streaked face.

Power had forgotten the plight of the Warrens while he relished the agony and death of Frank Snyder. Abruptly, as the woman shrieked her plea and he pushed two fresh shells into the shotgun, he started forward.

But Edge reached out and fastened a strong grip on the Negro's upper arm. Then jerked him back.

"She needs help!" Power snarled.

"She's got more than this town can handle right now," the half-breed drawled. "Go help the people, feller."

He released his hold on the black man, relinquishing responsibility for him. And lunged forward across the intersection. He ran down an alleyway with burning walls on either side, and then through the smoke that drifted across the back lots of the buildings on the west side of north Main Street. Twice braves loomed up through the smoke. Twice the Winchester's recoil jarred his arms and the Indians were flung over backwards.

Then he shot a white man. Out back of the bank, behind the advance of the Sioux. It was Cass Kerwin, who was holding three Indian ponies by their rope bridles. He went for his gun when he saw the tall, lean half-breed racing toward him. But was on his back with blood gushing from his mouth before he could half draw the Colt from the holster.

Edge threw himself down among the legs of the ponies as Nate and Tim Kerwin sprinted out of the burning bank. The brothers saw him and the dead Cass. But their hands were tight on bags of money.

"A share, Edge!" Nate roared.

"Ain't in the market," the half-breed growled, and shot the eldest Kerwin in the heart.

Tim hurled away his burdens, whirled, and ran. Into a searing wall of flames which had blocked the doorway.

As the man screamed and became a crumpling cinder of burnt flesh, Edge powered erect. The ponies scattered. The half-breed lunged forward, holding his breath against the smoke and heat. He scooped up all four sacks of money and backtracked toward the intersection.

There had been a lull in the gunfire at the center of town while Edge followed up his hunch about the missing Kerwins. He didn't trust the stillness that was disturbed only by the roaring of flames and crash of falling timbers. Using the smoke for cover, he swung wide of the intersection. He had been gone more than five minutes, but it was as if he had never left.

Laura Warren was still trying desperately to revive her unconscious husband in the center of the meeting of the streets. Conrad Power was still on the sidewalk in front of his hotel.

"I think they've gone, mister," he said without conviction as Edge appeared beside him.

"They scared of winning?" the half-breed growled.

The Negro swallowed hard. "What's that you got?"

"Guess you could say it was almost hot money." He joined Power in staring hard at the smoke which curtained three of the exits from the intersection. "The Kerwins hit the bank."

"The chopped chicken livers of this lousy place don't deserve that kinda help, mister," the Negro snarled, and spat. "I ain't gonna do nothin' to—"

Bullets thudded into the brickwork of the hotel wall.

Edge and Power threw themselves to the sidewalk. Laura Warren pressed herself harder against the unresponsive form of her husband.

There was smoke everywhere now. It veiled the sky and took the brightness from the sun. It hid most of the leaping flames which caused it.

But it did not conceal the advancing Sioux braves. They emerged from it like brightly painted wraiths, rifles at the ready. From the north section of Main Street and from both stretches of the cross street. Two dozen, or maybe thirty. Just as they had made the first slow advance on the town, so they kept their pace measured now. They were no longer venting war cries. But there was triumph clear to see on every daubed face. They were certain they had won. They had lost more than half their number, but it had been worth it. At the center of the line advancing from Main Street, Blue Moon was already dreaming of other towns that would soon be destroyed.

"The windows, Conrad," Edge growled.

"Yeah."

The braves held their fire, certain the two men on the sidewalk had died from the first volley. Laura Warren looked up and desperately around her. Then fell across Dan and sobbed. The Indians ignored the couple.

"Now!" Edge snapped.

He and Power sprang up, then lunged. Bullets smashed toward them. Both men crashed through the windows of the saloon. Their shoulders took the brunt of the impact against the glass. Their entire bodies were jarred as they hit the floor inside. There were a dozen separate fires in the saloon.

Edge zigzagged between the leaping flames, holding his breath, and came to a halt in the lobby of the hotel. Power was level with him the whole way. Both men

163

took hold of a door each and slammed it against the fires raging in the saloon.

A new barrage of gunfire exploded outside.

Voices were raised. But it was the whites who were giving full vent to war cries as the guns exploded.

The half-breed and the Negro exchanged glances, and sprinted across the lobby to peer out from either side of the open doorway. Across the platform with the body of Jody Tillson slumped on it, they saw a group of Democracy citizens had raced out into the open to face the Indians. From the south side of the intersection, with no one man in command, they traded bullets with the braves on the other three sides.

At the center, under the murderous crossfire, Laura pressed her sobbing body across the unmoving form of her husband.

"Maybe they're deservin' now, mister," Power yelled.

"One way or the other, looks like this is where it finishes, feller," Edge drawled in reply, and stepped into the doorway.

He fired from the hip, squeezing the trigger and pumping the lever action with cool, fast deliberation. The attackers of Democracy and its defenders fell. Dead or wounded. The wounded, if they were able, continued to loose bullets. Blue Moon was one of those who dropped to the ground and did not move again.

"This lousy shotgun!" Power growled angrily, moving out to stand beside Edge.

Both were protected by their own particular destiny from the flying death that came so close but never hit them.

The half-breed's rifle rattled empty. Before the final ejected shell flew out and bounced on the platform, it was over. The last of the braves went down. And he died with a curse venting from his gaping mouth.

All gunfire ceased.

Laura sobbed, then a harsh laugh was forced from her full lips as she heard Dan groan.

Edge shifted his gaze from the couple to the front of the stage line depot. His mare was on her side, an arrow protruding from an eye. But the gelding had survived. And the animal became still and quiet as a respite of relative peace descended over the burning town.

"You want to sell me your horse, feller?" Edge asked the Negro.

"He's yours. For free," Power offered absently.

"It's a good horse," Edge countered. "Nothing worthwhile is for nothing. I'll buy him."

"Suit yourself."

"Usually do."

The citizens of the town, who had regrouped in time to defeat the Sioux, started across the intersection. Their women and children trailed them. Amos Meek was there. So was McQuigg. Maggie Woodward. Edge moved along the sidewalk to retrieve the sacks of bank money. He wondered idly if all the politicians except Snyder had survived while the less unfluential citizens of Democracy made their stand. The Warrens looked at them, unable to find any words to say. The people ignored the couple. But there was no ill will yet. Toward the Warrens, the politicians, or the Indians. Toward the dead or the survivors. The shock was too deep.

Edge returned to the hotel doorway and, one by one, tossed the bulging sacks out onto the intersection, arcing them over the platform.

"What's the idea?" a man demanded.

"Money from the bank," Power supplied. "The Kerwins tried to steal it. Edge here stopped them."

"You think we care about money now?" a middle-aged woman cried, throwing her arms out to either side. "With the dead on the streets and the town burnin'?"

"Capital should be high on the list if you figure to rebuild Democracy," the half-breed said softly.

Only Power heard him. The people moved slowly off the intersection and down the smoke-filled streets in search of their loved ones and perhaps to see if they could salvage anything from the destroyed town.

Then, as the meeting of the streets was clear of everyone except the dead and Dan and Laura Warren, two gunshots cracked out.

The man was hit first, a perfect shot through the heart. Then the woman. Another heart shot. The two reports were so close together they almost sounded like one. And Laura had no time to scream her grief at her husband's death before she started to fall beside him.

Nobody reemerged from the smoke to see the reason for the shots. Perhaps they all knew and did not care.

Power groaned, then sighed. "Guess it's fittin', Mr. Edge," he said sadly. "It was them give the Sioux the chance to hit us."

"Happy you see it that way, Conrad," Gene Stanton said as he started down the stairway into the lobby hung with so many of his pictures.

Both the Negro and the half-breed had turned their backs on the intersection after seeing the Warrens die. For the shots had been aimed at the couple from the second floor of the hotel.

The lawman still had his ivory handled Beaumont-Adams in his fist as he descended the stairs. The gun was aimed at Edge.

"Figure you're all right, Conrad," the sheriff went on, his eyes as dead as they had ever been, his voice just loud enough to be heard above the crackling of the fires behind the closed doors of the saloon. "You didn't like us, but you fought clean until this stranger showed up. Way I used to fight before I decided I wanted more money than a lawman ever makes. But I'm still a good lawman. All I can be after the rest is all gone."

"Makes you feel full up inside, don't it, Edge?" Power said.

"Leaves me empty," the half-breed answered, moving his rifle almost imperceptibly.

Stanton had reached the foot of the stairway. At every tread down, he had adjusted his aim to keep the revolver pointing at the half-breed. He halted now.

"I was wrong, stranger. Wrong to throw in with Snyder and his crowd. Same as you was wrong to side with the Warrens. But mistakes get made. All the time. You made the biggest in lettin' a rusty old man get the drop on you."

The lips curled back to show the false dentures in a grin of evil triumph. The trigger finger was white-knuckled behind the guard.

"Stinkin' white trash!" Power snarled.

The dead eyes came to life with the fire of rage and switched their attention from one man to the other.

Edge released his hold on the empty Winchester. His palms stayed open and the Negro threw him the shotgun before the rifle hit the floor.

Both men in the doorway threw themselves to the floor. The revolver spat a bullet. It cracked across the dropping forms and smashed into the unfeeling face of the dead schoolteacher on the platform.

Both hammers of the shotgun were ready cocked. Edge's finger squeezed both triggers. Both barrels belched fire and shot. The gun was on its side. Sheriff Gene Stanton was peppered with flesh-tearing grains from belly to head. Skin, tissue, and tiny pieces of bone were ripped off of him and hurled in a crimson and white spray across the wall at the foot of the stairs. His mutilated body was flung against the wall, bounced off, and dropped to the floor.

"Obliged, Conrad," Edge said as he and the Negro got to their feet. He picked up the Winchester and handed the shotgun back to its owner.

"It sure was my pleasure," Power said, grinning. "So nothin' owed, uh?"

"Except for the horse."

"I'd really like you to take him for free, Mr. Edge. Somebody oughta get somethin' outta what happened here today. On top of good sense."

The half-breed had already peeled fifty dollars off the bankroll taken from his hip pocket.

"Somebody did, I figure," Edge answered, gesturing with the Winchester.

"Stanton?" Power said, bewildered. "What did that gent get except dead?"

"He was an artist, Conrad. He finally did what all of them want to."

The Negro saw that the rifle was pointing not to the bloodied corpse of the lawman. Instead, at a panoramic view of Democracy as it once had been, painted by the man who now lay dead beneath where it hung on the wall.

Power shook his head, uncomprehending. But he continued to peer at the painting, the vivid colors of which now seemed almost dull in contrast to the bright crimson of blood and pieces of pulpy tissue which had been sprayed across the canvas by the dying man. Then he sighed and looked at Edge. He saw that there was a sardonic smile on the lean, bristled face, glinting in the narrowed eyes and turning up the corners of the thin mouthline. "I don't get it."

"He did, feller. Got something of himself into a picture."

the Executioner

The gutsiest, most exciting hero in years.
Imagine a guy at war with the Godfather
and all his Mafioso relatives! He's rough,
he's deadly, he's a law unto himself —
nothing and nobody stops him!

THE EXECUTIONER SERIES by DON PENDLETON

Order		Title	Book #	Price
———	# 1	WAR AGAINST THE MAFIA	P401	$1.25
———	# 2	DEATH SQUAD	P402	$1.25
———	# 3	BATTLE MASK	P403	$1.25
———	# 4	MIAMI MASSACRE	P404	$1.25
———	# 5	CONTINENTAL CONTRACT	P405	$1.25
———	# 6	ASSAULT ON SOHO	P406	$1.25
———	# 7	NIGHTMARE IN NEW YORK	P407	$1.25
———	# 8	CHICAGO WIPEOUT	P408	$1.25
———	# 9	VEGAS VENDETTA	P409	$1.25
———	#10	CARIBBEAN KILL	P410	$1.25
———	#11	CALIFORNIA HIT	P411	$1.25
———	#12	BOSTON BLITZ	P412	$1.25
———	#13	WASHINGTON I.O.U.	P413	$1.25
———	#14	SAN DIEGO SIEGE	P414	$1.25
———	#15	PANIC IN PHILLY	P415	$1.25
———	#16	SICILIAN SLAUGHTER	P552	$1.25
———	#17	JERSEY GUNS	P328	$1.25
———	#18	TEXAS STORM	P353	$1.25
———	#19	DETROIT DEATHWATCH	P419	$1.25
———	#20	NEW ORLEANS KNOCKOUT	P475	$1.25
———	#21	FIREBASE SEATTLE	P499	$1.25
———	#22	HAWAIIAN HELLGROUND	P625	$1.25
———	#23	ST. LOUIS SHOWDOWN	P687	$1.25
———	#24	CANADIAN CRISIS	P779	$1.25
———	#25	COLORADO KILL-ZONE	P824	$1.25
———	#26	ACAPULCO RAMPAGE	P868	$1.25

TO ORDER
Please check the space next to the book/s you want, send this order form
together with your check or money order, include the price of the book/s
and 25¢ for handling and mailing to:
PINNACLE BOOKS, INC. / P.O. BOX 4347
Grand Central Station / New York, N.Y. 10017

☐ **CHECK HERE IF YOU WANT A FREE CATALOG**

I have enclosed $_____ check _____ or money order _____ as
payment in full. No C.O.D.'s.

Name _____

Address _____

City _____ State _____ Zip _____
(Please allow time for delivery.)   PB-38